By the same author

The Names of the Dead
Snow Angels
In the Walled City
On Writers and Writing by John Gardner (ed.)

THE SPEED QUEEN

Stewart O'Nan

VIKING

VIKING

Published by the Penguin Group
Penguin Books Ltd, 27 Wrights Lane, London W8 5TZ,
Penguin Books USA Inc., 375 Hudson Street, New York, New York 10014, USA
Penguin Books Australia Ltd, Ringwood, Victoria, Australia
Penguin Books Canada Ltd, 10 Alcorn Avenue, Toronto, Ontario, Canada M4V 3B2
Penguin Books (NZ) Ltd, 182–190 Wairau Road, Auckland 10, New Zealand

Penguin Books Ltd, Registered Offces: Harmondsworth, Middlesex, England

This edition first published in the USA by Doubleday 1997
Published in Great Britain by Viking 1997
1 3 5 7 9 10 8 6 4 2

Printed in Great Britain by Clays Ltd, St Ives plc

A CIP catalogue record for this book is available from the British Library
ISBN 0-670-87549-X

For my dear Stephen King

I suppose you'll call this a confession when you hear it.

– Raymond Chandler / James M. Cain
Double Indemnity

I been drivin' all night,
my hand's wet on the wheel.

– Golden Earring
'Radar Love'

THE SPEED QUEEN

SIDE A

TESTING, 1, 2, 3

I hope you don't mind but I wrote this first part out, so I'll just read it now and get it over with. Mr. Jefferies helped me with it. I hope that's okay.

Okay, let me just read it.

Before I begin I'd like to say that I'll try to remember everything as best as I can, though sometimes I know it won't be right. What you want to know about happened eight years ago, before I found the Lord. I was a different person then, a person I don't completely understand even now. That's not an excuse, nor is the drugs. I take full responsibility for the things that I did do—no more, no less. I maintain my innocence and consider my sentence unjust. I also think it's important for the public to know that legally I oppose capital punishment of any sort, not just in my own case.

Was that okay? You don't have to use it if you don't want to. Mr. Jefferies said we might put it right at the front of the book. He said you might want to cause it makes it more real—based on a true story, like. I don't know anything about writing a book, so anything like that is up to you. Mr. Jefferies said I should just do it to avoid any legal problems.

It's a novel, right? So it's supposed to be all made up. It should have a thing at the beginning like at the end of a movie—everyone in this isn't supposed to be alive or dead—even though everyone knows that's not true. I bet everyone asks you about Jack in *The Shining* and whether that's supposed to be you. You say no, I bet, or maybe he's just a little part of you. This'll be more like *Dolores Claiborne* meets *The Green Mile*, but still. As long as you say it's fiction and put that thing in, you're okay, you don't really have to answer that. But Mr. Jefferies said that that based-on-a-true-story thing is tricky, so I said, sure, let's put it in.

You probably already read Natalie's book. Let me just say here that very little of it's true, and none of the big things. I know why she said what she did, but it's not true. That's one reason I wanted you to do the book. After people read yours, no one'll believe hers.

Thank you for all the money. It's all going to go to Gainey when he's old enough. My mom won't see a penny of it, Mr. Jefferies said he'd see to it.

I like Mr. Jefferies. He's the only one who's done anything for me in this whole thing. I know he feels bad that we lost. I know he feels that *he* lost, but that's not true. We did the right thing, pleading not guilty. I *am* not guilty. He didn't know the judge was going to be so tough. You should have seen him right after we lost, he gave me this little hug anyway, but I could tell he thought it was his fault. And how can you tell someone it's not?

My mom says she would've paid for someone better. This is after the fact, of course. She's always generous when it's too late.

That part about being against the death penalty was Mr. Jefferies' idea. He's against it. Personally, I'm for it—which is funny cause I wasn't when I came in here. You meet people in here there's just nothing else to do with. It's like the Psalm says: *Preserve thou the righteous and let vengeance take the wicked.* And there is wickedness in the world, there are evil people, men and women both. But Mr. Jefferies, he's been working so hard for me I figure I owe it to him. It doesn't mean that much to me one way or the other.

Anyway, it's important for me to say all this before I begin. Mr. Jefferies said he'll listen to the tapes before he sends them to you, in case I say something illegal. He'll make one copy for you and one for Gainey when he's eighteen and keep this one for his records.

Legally, Mr. Lonergan and nobody on the staff are supposed to listen to these. I've got nothing against Mr. Lonergan, he's always been fair with my privileges, but this is private business. I know that legally you own these, but I'd appreciate it if you kept them to yourself. You can use it for your book because it's fiction but not for anything else. I know this is strange asking you this, since if things go the way they're going you can't really answer me, but if you could write to Mr. Jefferies with your answer I'd appreciate it.

I think that's it. Like you asked me, I didn't look at the questions ahead of time. There's a lot of them. I'll try to answer them as best I can before midnight. Janille is here but no one else, so there's no reason for me to be anything but honest. Sometimes I might not say what you want me to, but I'm just going to be honest. You can make up whatever story you want. I just want you to know the real one first.

1

Why did I kill them?

I didn't kill them. It's not even a question.

You think you'd start with something like my mom or dad or what I was like when I was a kid. Show me riding my tricycle out behind the chicken house, my hair in pigtails, buckteeth, something cute like that. Then you could say, she was a normal gal and look what happened to her. And you'd figure it out. You'd go back and look at everything that happened and say, look, it could happen to anyone.

But I'm glad it's you. When Mr. Jefferies said you bought the rights I didn't believe him. I was over on the Row then. Darcy next door said, "No!"

"Yep," I said, "it's true."

"No," she said.

I just nodded.

"What about Lamont?" she said, and I said you'd probably have to talk to his folks.

I'm sorry they didn't give you permission. Lamont would have wanted to be in the book. He liked your books. It's kind of a shame you'll have to change our names. It's dumb; everyone'll know it's us.

Why did I kill them?

I didn't kill them. I was there, but I didn't kill anyone.

I know exactly what happened though. It's pretty boring, actually. It's pretty normal. I don't think people will be that interested. But if anyone can make it interesting, you can. You'll make it funny too, which is right. Sometimes it was really funny. Even now some of it's funny.

I've read all your books. I know that sounds like Annie Wilkes in *Misery*, but it's true, really. I liked *Misery*. James Caan was really good in it. *Brian's Song* was on the other night. Janille rolled the set over so I could watch.

Janille's all right—right, Janille?

Janille and me get along all right except for Oprah. Janille can't stand that Oprah lost all that weight. Janille thinks she looked fine before the diet; I think she holds it against her. I think Oprah's someone who tried to change herself and succeeded, and I respect that in a person. We fight about this all the time. We could both stand to lose a few pounds. It's all that junk from the vending machines. We'll take a break—that's what Janille calls it—and have some Funyuns and an RC, or split a Payday when we're being really bad. This is usually around "All My Kids" or "One Life to Live." Definitely before Oprah.

I kind of rely on TV in here, that and the Bible. Tonight they say I can watch as much as I want. I can order anything I want to eat. I can pretty much do anything I want. They say I can have a sedative about four hours before. The last gal they did here took it—the famous one, Connie Something, the gal who cut up all those truckers. By midnight she was just a mess, all crying and her feet going all over the place. They had to carry her in.

Janille doesn't know this, but Darcy slipped me three white crosses before they moved me over here. I've been saving them for tonight. I figure what the heck, I've got to do this thing for you. I'm going to do them right after dinner. I'll tell you when they kick in. You'll probably be able to tell anyway.

That was my nickname in the papers—the Speed Queen. I've always moved a little faster than the rest of the world. That's why I'm here, I guess. I don't always stop to think, I just want to go. Lamont used to say I was built for speed. It's true; the world's always seemed a little slow to me. It's chemical, I think. Everything I used to do just fed into that. When I was using, I didn't have to eat or sleep or anything, just get in that Roadrunner and go. Now I've got a few things that calm me down. My relationship with Jesus, obviously. Gainey. Knowing I've only got so much time left. I think I always knew I'd hit some kind of wall. It's like that movie *Vanishing Point*, the guy out there in the desert in that big old Challenger, just hauling around with Cleavon Little on the radio. In the end he hits the blade of this bulldozer and the car just rips into flames, little pieces of sheet metal falling in slow motion like snow. That's the kind of life I wanted back then. I guess I got it, huh?

I've been over here twice before. The Death House. Actually it's kind of nice. The mattresses are new, and the walls don't sweat like the old ones. Two-tone—light gray over dark gray, the line right at neck level. Steel john, steel mirror. The only bad thing is there's no windows. It drives Janille crazy.

The last time I got my stay early in the morning, the time before that around dinnertime. My dinner was already here, so they let me have it anyway—barbecue from Leo's, the ribs crusty, sliding right off the bone. Say what you like about Oklahoma, but the barbecue is amazing here. That and the gas is cheap.

They use lethal injection here. It's kind of disappointing. New Mexico used to use the chair but then they changed to it too. Mr. Jefferies made sure we came here; he thought the publicity would kill us in New Mexico.

Kill us—it's a joke.

Remember Foghorn Leghorn? *That's a joke, son.* I never thought he was funny until Lamont and me did some bong hits in bed one morning and he turned on the cartoons. He smelled good in bed, that's what I always remember about Lamont. He was always good to me that way. He used to kiss me right on my heart.

Lamont taught me a lot. Some of it was good. I won't pretend like it wasn't.

I wish it was the chair. The chair makes me think of heaven. It's like a throne.

The table for the injection's shaped like a gingerbread man. It's got ten straps.

It's not the needles I mind. My veins are better than they've been since high school, thick as worms. Everyone says it's supposed to be like going to sleep. It's not going to be like that. I don't know what it's going to be like. Last night I pictured it was like flushing your radiator and putting in new antifreeze. They say the gal who killed those truckers broke two of the straps—and those are new straps. But it sounds good to most people, sleep.

Sister Perpetua said there were four stages I had to go through. She wrote them down for me—denial, anger, grief, acceptance. She was right, kind of. Since I've been here I've been through all of them. The problem is, one stage doesn't just end and then the next one kicks in. They get all mixed up with each other. They're all going at the same time.

Why did I kill them is something I'd expect from Barbara Walters or someone. You're not going to start there, are you? You think you'd start at the beginning—not with me as a little girl but maybe when I hooked up with Lamont. Because we had a year or so there before Natalie came along. Good times. We were both working and Lamont bought that Hemi Roadrunner. We used to cruise Sooner from the big Sonic down around the Whataburger, just snuggling up on that bench seat with the Ramones grinding out a wall of sound, jumbo cherry slushes in the cup holders. You could start there and show how much we were in love and how normal we were and then how everything went wrong. That's what I'd do.

2

Lamont used the gun first because he had to. It was an old Colt he got from a dealer in Midwest City. He traded him a patched-up gas tank from a '70 Torino. It had an eight-round clip and the kind of safety on the back of the grip you had to hold down with the meat of your thumb. It kicked so hard the first time I fired it that the hammer put a dent in my forehead.

You can get all of that from the police reports. You're just testing me, like the questions at the beginning of a lie detector test. I've done some of those, and I'll tell you, they don't all work.

I think what I'm going to do is answer the questions in order and then maybe when I'm all done put them in the order I think they should go in. Cause right now this is backwards. The important thing isn't whether I killed them or how, it's everything. My whole life really. That's what you paid for, isn't it?

He used the gun first and then Natalie used the knife. I don't really see the difference. I didn't use either of them anyway.

And it's a dumb question. How could *I* use the knife first?

There were five of them and one of me, and back then I weighed like a pound.

Not that it was self-defense at that point. Mr. Jefferies said it was going to be murder even though I didn't do it. The question was, was it second degree or first, and how many counts of each? That's not even including the Closes and all of that.

But that should go later. First I think you'd want to talk about me growing up in the country. In the newspaper no one ever mentions I'm from the country, and I think it's interesting.

My family was my mom, my dad and me, and our dog, Jody-Jo. He was a basset hound the color of a Fudgsicle except where he'd turned white. He was old and had bad dandruff and farted a lot. He didn't like to play with you. He'd just lie under the glider, and when you wanted to rock, he'd get up and say something before he walked off. His back legs moved kind of sideways. He was my mom's dog from before they got married, and my dad refused to clean up after him. My mom had a shovel around the side of the garage, and a trash bag.

The house though. You ever see *Bonnie and Clyde*? It was just like that. The next house was a mile down the road on each side. This was right on Route 66, the old one. All day I'd sit on the glider and watch the cars come by; my dad taught me all the names—Chieftain and Starfire, Rocket 88. The nearest town was Depew. In back we had an old chicken house and back behind that a pond the dirt turned red. The house was yellow and had two floors. I don't remember any of the furniture except a piano that was always broken. You'd hit a key and nothing happened.

The wind was the big thing there. It really did come sweeping down the plain. I don't know if you've ever been out here, but don't forget to put that in the book. Make it windy like every other day. You could say it's windy tonight, that all those protesters outside the gate are getting their signs and coffee cups blown around. Or say I can hear it whistling around the Death House like a ghost. Something like that, just get it in, you know how to do it.

Out there the big worry was tornadoes. April and May was the season. If you saw one, you were supposed to call the police in Depew, then open your windows a crack and wait in the basement. We had an old mattress down there, and when the warning came on the radio, my mom would take me and Jody-Jo down and we'd sit on the mattress and eat Ritz crackers with peanut butter until the radio said it was okay. Depew had a siren; on a calm day you could barely hear it. But I never saw one. All I remember is every few days the wind would take one of my mom's sheets off the line and dip it in the pond and she'd fish it out, cursing like you never heard.

There weren't any chickens left in the chicken house, just dust from the feathers that made you sneeze and a smell like ammonia. Behind the house was a little hill I'd ride my tricycle down. I'd pedal as fast as I could and then when the pedals were going too fast to catch up with I'd hold my feet out and let the pedals go crazy. I used to fall off a lot. When I went inside, my mother would slap the dirt off my dress. It was kind of like a spanking. "What have you been doing?" she'd say. "Haven't I told you a million times not to do that? What's wrong with you?"

My tricycle had plastic tassels that came out of the handgrips. You could hang on to them like reins. You couldn't steer so good with them, but that made it more exciting.

When I was four I broke my wrist. I was riding down the hill when the front wheel hit this dip. The wheel turned and I went over the handlebars and the trike came down on top of me. I thought I was fine. I was used to that kind of thing. I got up and tried to pick the trike up, but my hand wouldn't do what I was telling it. I went inside and told my mom.

"What did I tell you?" she said. "I told you but you wouldn't listen to me, would you? Now do you see what happens?"

And I *didn't* listen to her. They put a cast on my wrist that my fingers stuck out of, and when I came back I got right back on my tricycle. A few days later I had the exact same accident again, except this time the cast hit me in the side of the head and completely knocked me out. I woke up a little later and went inside. I didn't tell anyone, but in bed that night I could hear like a radio in my head, just soft so you couldn't make out what they were saying.

I know what you're thinking but it's not true. I was better the next day. I've never heard any other voices. If you want to do something with that, then fine, but that's not my story, that's yours.

If you do, you might say it was the spirit of a Pawnee squaw. A few years ago some people from the university dug up a whole ditchful of bones near Depew. They think it was a massacre that got covered up. You might say it was the sole survivor's ghost coming back to find her husband and babies. (You could do it in parentheses or *italics* so we'd know it was a voice in her head, like in *Pet Sematary*.)

We lived on Route 66 until I was five, when my dad got a job at Remington Park and we moved closer to Oklahoma City. I was excited about moving, but sad too, leaving the pond and the chicken house, the little hill.

I guess I should take this time to apologize to the Close family. Lamont and me are honestly sorry for causing them all such pain, and I wish I could undo what's done. I can't. I hope my death will be some comfort to their family. I'd like them to know that we had nothing against Marla and Terry Close, and that they were not involved with the drug business or anything illegal, like the newspapers say. They just happened to be living in that house at that time. As a Christian I pray they've found their reward just as I hope to find mine tonight.

That was one thing I noticed when we were there that last

time—the piano was gone. I thought something that heavy would never move, I don't know why. It was a shock. I remember saying something to Lamont when we were tying them up.

"What?" he said, because the kerosene was splashing.

"The piano," I said, "it's gone."

And he stopped what he was doing and asked me where it used to be.

"Right here," I said, and made the shape of it with my hands.

Lamont put his arm around me, and we stood there looking at where it should have been. There was a bookcase there with pictures of the Closes. They were on a beach somewhere with a sunset lighting up the sky, drinking those little drinks with umbrellas. Behind us, Mrs. Close was whimpering inside the trash bag. Mr. Close's hand was still flipping like a fish.

"What the heck," I said, "the thing never worked anyway," and we went back to work.

We sat on the couch and watched them a little bit, then got on the road. When we passed Depew, the siren was going wild.

3

I'm not going to say anything about the number of times. You can get that from the newspapers. I'm sorry about that now, but after the fifth or sixth time they probably didn't feel anything. That's not what I will or won't be forgiven for anyway. That was Natalie.

I understand you need all these details to tell the story right, that people are interested in that kind of thing. I don't know why we did it. Everyone asks me that. All I can tell you is that sometimes you just go off, you don't know when to stop. Later you come back to yourself, but sometimes you just go off to this other place.

I'm not explaining it right.

I remember doing it. It's not like I wasn't there or that I wasn't the one doing it. It's like nothing else existed except me. Does that make sense? I was the only one that counted. They were there just to please me, to make me count more. The more I did it, the bigger I got. It's a drug by itself, the size you get.

I'll try to answer that better later on. It's a hard one.

We moved from outside Depew to Kickingbird Circle in Edmond. It was a new development then, the houses were brand-new, with just dirt for yards, stakes with strings between them. The city was still building the streetlights; the gutters were filled with nuts and bolts. It was like a play where they're still building the set.

My dad was an assistant trainer at Remington Park, and my mom worked at the local post office. That's right, the one where the guy barricaded the doors and shot everyone. I figured you'd like that. Maybe you could make her the only survivor who has these bad dreams and tells me about hiding in a canvas cart. But she'd quit by then. By then she'd made her pension and stayed home all day reading mysteries and listening to the radio.

She doesn't read your books. She likes the ones where you get the same lady detective except they're working on a different case. It's like a TV series, you get the same characters over and over. Like "Cheers"—you know everybody. She goes through two or three a week. She gets them from the library.

When she heard you were going to do the book, she said, "Anyone but him."

I said, "Mom, what do you want, he's the biggest writer in America."

"He'll do a job on you," she says. "He'll make you look bad."

So just for me, make me look okay, all right?

Anyway, we lived on Kickingbird Circle and I went to school at Northern Hills elementary. My mom gave me a key so I could get in after school, and she'd always leave me cookies or grapes or a note that said there were Popsicles in the freezer and I could have one if I took it outside. I'd watch "Speed Racer" and maybe "Gilligan's Island" or go over to Clara Davies' house and play Barbies or Mystery Date or whatever. Then around five-thirty my mom would pull her Toronado into the drive and ten minutes later my dad would roll up in his Continental, and I'd help make dinner.

It was normal. I had friends. I liked school, especially geography. I belonged to the Glee Club. In gym I was the best at the softball throw. You can check up on all of this and everyone will tell you it's true. It wasn't like *Carrie* at all. My shoes were new; no one laughed at my clothes.

The only strange thing about my childhood is that we didn't go to church. Not once. I don't know why that was, maybe because Sunday was a big day at the track. My dad would get up like any other workday and back the Continental out and take off while the rest of Kickingbird Circle was still asleep. Later my mom would make pancakes and we'd read the paper together at the kitchen table. We read everything, even the stupid cartoons in *Parade* magazine. Our fingers turned gray.

I can hear you thinking it was too normal, it was weird normal. Not true. No one said it was perfect. We wanted to believe that, I think—the kids—but we knew it wasn't true. Mrs. Richardson had a stroke and they moved away. Darryl Marshall ran over Tallulah, the Underwoods' Siamese. It was mysterious, I guess, because we all crowded around, but I wasn't the one who picked it up with a stick, and that night I didn't worry about it. Before bed I looked out my window at the far-off lights of the city and up at the stars and made the same wish I always did—that my life would always be like this.

4

This is better.

I met Lamont Standiford for the first time on Friday, October 26th, 1984. I was working the swing shift at the Conoco on the Broadway Extension. I was drinking then. Every night I drank a fifth of vodka. As long as you smoked, they couldn't smell it on you. It was a good job for an alcoholic. All I had to do was punch buttons and accept money. I'd been working there a month and I'd already gotten a dollar raise.

He was driving a firemist-red 442 convertible with a black top. I'd seen the car cruising Broadway; there wasn't much to do but look out the window. He pulled up to pump 7 and the light on my board came on. He waved at me to turn the pump on. I hit the button. It was like being a lab rat; the light comes on, you hit the button. Sometimes the customers get angry when you're slow. Not him. He waved to say thank you, and I gave him a smile. He was smoking right next to the No Smoking sign. He was slim in black cigarette-leg jeans and his hair was all over the place, like he'd been riding with the top down. He bent over to fit the nozzle in. I was drunk and I'd just broken up with Rico and I thought it might be nice to have somebody again.

I had a customer to take care of, so I put down my cigarette and made change for them, and then somebody else. When I was done I sat back on my stool and took a drag. I couldn't see him. I thought he'd flipped down his license plate to fill up, but I couldn't see him. I stood up for a better look and saw that he didn't have a license plate, and right then he pulled out and across traffic and I lost him in the stream of taillights.

For every drive-off you had to fill out a form. The more you had, the harder the manager looked at your receipts. Each one made you remember what a crummy job you had. I hit the reset for 7 and started filling it out. I hated seeing my handwriting going all over the place. By then I was tired of being a drunk but there wasn't anything else I could do. I got down to Description of Vehicle and thought how easy it would be to find a car like that, and I started to put down the wrong car. I'd only seen him for a minute but I started to put down a Buick Skylark.

And right when I'm finishing the description, the 442 pulls in again. It's got the grabber hood with rally stripes, raised white letter tires, spinner hubs—nothing fancy, just very tasteful. It pulls right up in front of my window and out he gets. He swings his hair back out of his eyes and bends down to the hole in the Plexiglas, and his pupils are huge. He has these teeth that are almost fangs. I like his eyebrows, the way they bend down at the ends.

"I forget what number I was on," he says, and slides a twenty into the trough.

"Lucky seven," I say.

"Yeah," he says, surprised I know, and looks at me.

I can still bring back that look—his eyes like an eclipse, the way his hair blew around his face, how he hooked a piece out of his mouth with a pinky.

"Nice ride," I said, and I think we knew. Sometimes love doesn't take much. You just have to be there when it shows up.

My dad wanted to be a jockey but he was too tall. He was just over five feet, and by the time I knew him he was heavy. He wore a different-colored windbreaker to work every day, all with his name over his heart—Phil. I never called him anything except Dad, but my friends would say, "How's old Phil doing?" or "When's Phil getting home?"

He used to pick me up and swing me by the ankles. I'd ask

him all the time. "Swing me," I'd say, "swing me." He stood in the middle of the living room, spinning to keep up with me. One time he must of gotten dizzy because my head went right into the side of the TV console. I went right out, and when I came to I was on the couch with a towel under my head. My dad had ice in a washcloth. There was blood on it, watered down. He didn't seem worried. He'd probably done this a lot at work.

He was saying my name but I could barely hear him. Something was humming. The ice came down like he was going to put it in my eye.

"Margie," he said. "Margie."

Every time I could hear it a little better, like the humming was melting away.

My mom came in from the garden; she had dirty gloves on. "What happened?" she asked, and my father told her. He showed her the washcloth.

She came over and looked down at me. I tried to smile.

"She'll be all right," she said.

At dinner, I fell asleep in my chair. My dad said I just fell right off it. At the hospital the doctor said I had a fractured skull.

On the way home I sat between them in the front seat. My dad was too upset to drive, and my mom kept reaching over me to stroke the back of his neck.

"It's just a hairline," she said. "Phil, she'll be fine."

5

My mom didn't think anything about Lamont. When I met him, I was living with two of my girlfriends in a bungalow behind the library in Edmond—Garlyn and Joy. This was after Rico and me broke up. My mom wasn't talking to me for a lot of reasons I'll get into later.

Garlyn and Joy made a place for me. We were all drinking and going through a lot of jobs. But the place was clean, that was one thing we were careful about. Most of our furniture was plants because Joy had a talent for it. We'd all get up around noon and zombie around the house, cleaning up in slow motion. Garlyn had a crate of old blues records and we'd get stoned and eat cereal on the couch and listen to Lightnin' Hopkins and Sonny and Brownie.

It's funny, half the songs were these guys in prison for murder. They'd be hooting and hollering stuff like *I done killed my woman / don't you know she done me wrong*. They weren't sorry exactly, more like they'd learned something from it, like they wouldn't make the same mistake again. We'd make up our own verses. *I done paid that electric bill / I done paid it yesterday*. Joy would sing into a beer bottle like it was a microphone and do Janis Joplin or put on a pair of shades for John Belushi. She could do all these dead people. We respected people like that, who'd killed themselves having a big time. We were like them except we weren't famous yet, or dead.

That was the best part of the day then, before we had to get ready for work. We'd sit there drinking and singing until someone said, "It's that time." That might be a good place for some wind—when we leave the house in our uniforms. We all had to wear one. Joy worked the drive-in window at Taco Mayo; Garlyn had just moved to Crockett's Smoke House. I'd been at the Conoco only a month or so, and I knew that wasn't going to last because I'd already started stealing.

I'd steal cartons of Marlboros and sixes of 3.2 beer. In the beginning it was mostly for myself. Later when I knew I was going to quit, I'd fill up a trash bag and toss it in the dumpster for Lamont to pick up. Another thing I took was gum. We always had lots of gum—Bubble Yum, Bubblicious, Wrigley's, Care Free. I'd bring it home in my purse. It was good because I felt like

I was doing my part for the house. We all needed it, especially on the job.

That's how Lamont got to know me; he'd take me home after my shift. The first time he offered I knew he was going to because he'd cruised through the lot twice. He came in around ten to eleven and parked by the air pump. By then I'd finished my bottle and I was feeling all right. At home I had another pint in the freezer, hidden in a box of frozen peas. It was a good time of the night.

He waited until Mister Fred Fred, the graveyard guy, came in. You'd love Mister Fred Fred, he's a whole book in himself. They hired him as part of this outpatient placement thing the state was doing. He was basically nuts. He had this notebook he was filling up with scientific formulas to prove something about the planets. He showed me the diagram once. All the planets were lined up right in line with Oklahoma City—really with Mister Fred Fred. In a circle in a corner there was a smaller diagram showing this lightning bolt going through his head. He was trying to prove the planets were doing something to him, that they were against him somehow. I don't know what he thought anyone was going to do about it if he actually proved it.

I gave Mister Fred Fred his name. Really he gave it to himself, I was just there when he did it. This counselor guy brought him over from Nancy Daniels, this group home. All he had to do to get the job was fill out this application. Stan the manager brought him in the back of the booth to do it. His hair wasn't completely combed, it was kind of fluffed up in back like he'd been sleeping on it. The counselor guy was saying everyone thought Fred was ready for this big step and how generous it was of us and everything, and meanwhile Fred is filling out the form all by himself. I go in back to get a box of Milky Ways, and on my way out I look over his shoulder. The only thing he's filled out is his name. He's circled *Mr.* First name: *Fred*; last name: *Fred.* The rest is blank.

That first night Lamont drove me home, Mister Fred Fred came in with his notebook. All he ever said was hello; after that it was like you weren't there. I always said a little extra, thinking it might trigger something. Now remember Mister Fred Fred, because he comes back later.

So I close out my register and sign the tape and slip it into the safe. Mister Fred Fred is already ringing people up. "Good night," I say real loud, and go outside and wait for Garlyn to pick me up.

But I'm not really waiting for her, I'm waiting for Lamont to come over and offer me a ride. I like that he doesn't right away. The 442 has tinted glass; under the lights the purple turns black, you can't see a thing.

Then he starts the car. It's like an animal, it makes my heart jump. The lights shine right on me. It's silly—I already want him—but it's sweet.

He pops the clutch and the 442 leaves a streak. It lunges and then stops right in front of me, the exhaust popping. I still can't see anything through the windows.

The passenger door swings open, letting out some vintage MC5. It's like high school, I'm thinking, but so what?

I look around one last time for Garlyn, then get in.

His eyes are the same as the other night, just sucking me in. He smiles and gives me those fangs of his.

"So," he says. "Where you want to go?"

I forgot to tell you about Jody-Jo. He didn't make it to Edmond with us. One day he laid down under the glider and died. Nobody noticed until after supper. Usually he'd clean up under the table by licking the rug. It was disgusting. My mom called him but he didn't come. She found him under the glider and thought he was asleep. She stuck her foot under and pushed his shoulder. She did it again, then knelt down.

"Get your father," she said.

My dad came out and put one hand on Jody-Jo's neck, like he was trying to take his pulse.

"It doesn't look good," he said.

My mom was hugging herself, holding her elbows like she was cold. I remember that because she did the same thing at my trial.

My dad got up and held her. "He lived a long life," he said, like it was an accomplishment for a dog. He squeezed her and then turned her toward the door, an arm over her shoulder, and I could see he wanted us to all go inside.

My mom went in to finish the dishes while I watched TV. This was way before cable, and out near Depew there wasn't much of a choice of stations. Outside, the glider clanked and screeched. There was some nature show on — animals eating each other — and I went to the front window to see if I could see my dad.

He was wearing my mom's gardening gloves. He had a big trash bag he was trying to stuff Jody-Jo into. He had the twist tie in his teeth. Jody-Jo's back legs kept flopping out. My dad lifted the bag off the floor to get him all in, then closed the mouth, spun it around and fastened the tie. The bag held air like a balloon. When he set it down it toppled over. He threw the gloves on the glider and lit a cigarette, then after a few hits tossed it into the yard. He grabbed the stem of the bag and dragged it across the floorboards. Before he made it to the stairs, it ripped, and one of Jody-Jo's legs fell out. My dad saw it but didn't stop. He bumped the bag down the stairs and hauled it across the yard all the way to the road, where he leaned it against some other bags. Then he came back and put the glider back where it was supposed to go and brought my mom's gloves in.

That morning the county garbage truck woke me up, the back of it grinding. I went to my window and watched its lights blinking. The two guys riding the back had sweatshirts with hoods on. They threw the bags in and climbed on again and the truck pulled away.

At breakfast my mom said Jody-Jo was buried behind the chicken house. Later we took some flowers out. My mom stuck them in the turned dirt like they might grow.

"Dad put him in the trash," I said. "The garbage truck squished him."

"How many times do I have to tell you?" she said. "If you keep making up stories, no one's going to believe anything you say."

I know that's not really interesting, but a year before that, my dad hit Jody-Jo with my mom's car. It was an accident. Jody-Jo liked to run out and jump around my mom's car when she came home, like he was saying hi. This particular day my dad's old Polara was in the shop, so he was driving the Toronado, and Jody-Jo thought it was her. What Jody-Jo did was he'd run right at her car and she'd stop and he'd come around to her window and give her a kiss. So when the Toronado pulled in he ran right at it. My dad must have thought Jody-Jo would swerve at the last second, because he ran right over him. My dad said he heard a thump and then stopped. Jody-Jo was okay though, he just had a big knot on his head.

Maybe you could put those two things together. They were both accidents, but my dad really didn't like him. I don't know, it's just a suggestion. You know what you're doing, I don't.

6

No, I hadn't done that many drugs before Lamont. I was pretty conservative. I smoked weed all through high school but everyone does that. Drank beer, a little vodka, just on the weekends. It was pretty tame. I used to do downs when I could get them—Percodan, Percocet, bootleg Quaaludes. Percocet and gin used to be my favorite. I could watch TV for hours that way. Saturdays we'd go over to Mary Alice Tompkins' house and watch the Sooners destroy somebody. By halftime it didn't even matter. But that was just fun stuff, things kids do.

I did a little acid, five or ten trips in all. It was mostly speed, I think. You'd sweat something terrible and your fingers would go cold. You'd drop before homeroom and cut the rest of the day and when you got home you'd still be going and you'd have to force yourself to eat. I remember spreading my food around on my plate to make it look like I did. I'm sure my mom thought I was anorexic. Getting up the next day was always tough.

So no, not really. I was pretty straight.

I drank a lot. No one ever says anything about that. It's the Speed Queen thing. It started when I was living by myself. I was going to the university during the day and working at Mister Swiss nights.

Mister Swiss was an old Tastee-Freez made up to look like a chalet. You had to dress up like a milkmaid. All the burgers were named after the Alps; the double-decker was the Matterhorn. The big thing was the sundaes, which they called Avalanches. The manager made you say these things. You couldn't say, "Double cheeseburger," you had to say, "Matterhorn." It was on a speaker so everyone in the place could hear you. Everything

they made was fried—burgers, rings, chicken and shrimp baskets. Every other day you had to drain the Fry-o-lator and take
the bucket of grease to a special dumpster out back. There was a
big grease spot on the parking lot, and when it rained you didn't
dare step on it. After your shift, you felt like you'd been dipped in
oil.

I got home around midnight and I'd take a cold beer into the
shower with me. It was my reward for making it through the day.
I'd have another while I dried my hair, and then one watching
Letterman, and pretty soon I was sleeping in and missing class.

I got put on probation and my mom said she wouldn't help
me pay for classes unless I started doing better, but the next
semester was worse. I took some summer classes and did all right,
but that fall I got sick and fell behind and just stopped going. I
forgot to withdraw, so I got all F's. My mom said that was it, my
dad wouldn't have wanted her to throw any more money away. It
didn't really matter that much to me; I was only going because
he'd wanted me to. It was easier not to. Now all I had to do was
go to work.

You might say I was going to school to be an artist or a writer
or something. That might be interesting. I never really declared a
major, so technically it wouldn't be untrue. All I took were some
business courses—statistics and economics, boring stuff. You
could make me a painter, and I'd paint weird, runny pictures of
my dad or the house near Depew, or Jody-Jo, or my tricycle out
behind the chicken house. I could go inside my paintings, like in
Rose Madder. I'd meet this other painter from New York City or
Paris, and we'd have this unbreakable bond. All we'd do is drink
wine and make love by candlelight, and then he'd be killed somehow or die of some rare disease, and I'd start drinking more wine
and painting him over and over until I couldn't stand it. I could
break a mirror with a bottle and I'd look just like one of my

paintings, all runny and weird. Then I'd burn all my paintings and quit Mister Swiss and go work the drive-thru at Schlotzky's and meet Rico.

Another thing about Jody-Jo is that he had a house. It was under the one tree in the front yard and had actual shingles on the roof. After he was dead, I'd sit in it and spy on the cars driving by. My dad taught me all the names—Javelin, Montego, Wildcat. You could still smell Jody-Jo; there was a dark ball of hair in one corner. Sometimes I'd close my eyes and pretend I was him. My mom said that he'd gone to heaven, and I wanted to go there too. I couldn't picture what it looked like, I could only see Jody-Jo walking this white path surrounded by cotton-ball clouds. Then I'd see the trash bag and his legs going into the cruncher and I had to open my eyes.

My mom wanted another dog but my dad said no. It got to be a kind of joke between them, like when she saw a puppy on TV, but they were both serious. When my dad died, my mom went down to the Animal Rescue League and got Stormy. It's funny, she never said my dad went to heaven.

Where am I going to go? I know you'll ask that later. But in case I don't make it to the end, let me say now that I'm going to heaven. I'm a prayer warrior, and I've had to fight my own evil heart to get there. If Jody-Jo and my dad are there, I'll give them both a big hug. But I don't want to live with them again. I'd like to have a place with Lamont if that's possible, and if for whatever reason it isn't, then I'd like a place of my own.

Hang on, Janille wants something.

Yeah?

Double on the hot links, double on the beans. And lots of sauce. The hot.

Hold the Texas Toast, or you can have it.

Gimme the regular. I think it's too late for the diet.

Sorry. That was Leo's double-checking my order. Last time they forgot the brisket, and Janille let them hear about it. You like barbecue? You should come out here. I could take you some places.

The Last Supper, right? I'm sure you can do something with that. I'll have to stop the machine for that. You've got to concentrate on good barbecue.

I think I saw an "Outer Limits" where this guy who's going to the chair asks for this impossible last meal. He just keeps ordering and the cooks keep bringing the food and he's eating and eating and getting bigger and bigger until he's too big for the cell, and the bars bend and the concrete cracks and he breaks out. He's as big as Godzilla, and the guards in the towers are shooting at him, but he kicks right through the wall. In the end it's all a dream he's having while he's in the chair. You see him jerking. Rod Serling or whoever is talking about how a man finally becomes free and they zoom in on the guards unbuckling the straps. When they do that to me, I'll have hot sauce under my nails.

7

What do you mean by evaluated? I was tested in New Mexico when they caught me, but I was never committed or anything. Mr. Jefferies said everybody gets those tests. He said we wouldn't use it as a defense because of the judge.

There are some people here who think I'm crazy and there are some people here who think I did all of it. A lot of them are the same people. I can see why they'd think that, the way they were all cut up. I heard that Sonic took all their ads off the air right after that.

I'm not saying that wasn't me, just that I wasn't the only one.

I wasn't the one who started it and I wasn't the one who planned it in the first place; I was just there. When you're there and it's happening, you don't say, "Wait, this is crazy." It's different just sitting somewhere and thinking about it; you think you'd never do it. Then you're there and you do and there's nothing at all crazy about it.

Those tests are like lie detectors, you can't trust them. They're easy to trick; you just pretend you're someone else.

When I was a kid I used to think I was crazy. I thought I was the only one who could talk inside my head. I'd sit inside Jody-Jo's house and talk to myself.

"Dad put him in a bag," my inside voice said.

"Mom said he buried him," I said. It was like two people talking.

"Dig him up and see."

"With what?" I said.

Sometimes my inside voice would surprise me and say things I didn't know—like the guy in *The Waste Lands*. It would say things I know *I* didn't think.

"With the pitchfork," it said. "With Mom's garden shears."

"It was just a story," I said.

"With your hands."

"Dad wouldn't do that."

"You're just afraid to find out."

But everybody does that. It's not like voices, it's just the way people think. I used to think it made me crazy. No one told me different, and I wasn't going to ask.

In eighth grade they gave me a test to see what I was best at, one of those ones where you're supposed to describe yourself. You'd say what you'd do if this or that happened to you, like *You find out your friend Mary has been spreading lies about you. What do you do? (A) Confront her. (B) Say nothing.* and other stuff like that.

They wanted to see if you'd be a good waitress or something. I was stoned, so I just filled in all the A's.

The next week I got called down to Mrs. Drake, the school counselor. She had posters on her walls of seagulls with poetry on them and ivy plants spilling over her desk. She took her glasses off to talk to me.

"Marjorie," she said, "I was looking over the scores and yours jumped right out at me."

"I just wrote down all the A's," I said.

"Now why did you do that?"

"I don't know," I said.

"Have you ever had a problem with anger or aggression?"

"No," I said, hoping she didn't know about my fight on the bus with Shona Potts.

The week before I'd made fun of Shona's new glasses. Getting off at her stop, Shona pointed at me and said, "See ya tomorrow, Marge the Barge," and everyone laughed. The next morning when she got on, I snuck up the aisle till I was sitting right behind her. Everyone knew what I was going to do. Her hair was held in stiff pigtails by red rubber bands. I rolled my sleeve up and made a fist like my dad taught me, making sure my thumb was outside of my fingers. I reached my elbow back as far as the seat would let me and punched her in the side of the head. Her new glasses flew over the rows. Later they said that Shona would have double vision from it, but at the time I thought I'd let her off easy. I didn't hit her that hard; it didn't even hurt my hand.

I got suspended but didn't tell my mom. I'd ride the bus in and hang out around the auditorium. For a while no one talked to me. At lunch, people winged their salt packets at me, and once an empty chocolate-milk carton that spotted my blouse. I'd come home and go to my room and sit on my bed with the sun going down. My mom didn't understand what was happening. What kind of school was I going to?

Mrs. Drake wanted me to retake the test and a bunch of other ones, and I did. I did fine. They were easy. The big one said I would enjoy a career helping other people.

8

I have no idea what my IQ is. In grade school I got B's and C's, and then C's and D's in high school. I didn't like high school, the teachers made me feel stupid. I didn't see the point. I learned more from watching TV and reading books. My dad had really wanted me to go to college, so I did. Lamont used to call me his college girl. I liked that at first.

I've gotten smarter since I've been here. That's one good thing, it gives you time to think. In the morning one of the trusties rolls the book cart around and you get to pick one. They've got all of yours, but they're always out. The last one I read was an old one — *Cujo*. I think I liked it, how the rabies made this regular dog into a monster. At first I thought it would be stupid — I mean, who's really afraid of a dog? — but it was good. You could almost believe something like that could happen.

The cart's got everything: Danielle Steel, Mary Higgins Clark — all the good ones. Sometimes the good parts are missing, like when you cut coupons out of the newspaper, but I like filling things in on my own.

You're allowed two books of your own here, and one has to be religious. Besides the Bible, I have my road atlas. *Discover America!* the cover says. I lie on my bunk and drive all across the country. I just pick a road and go.

I read the Bible every day. Not much, just a page or so. When Sister Perpetua comes, we talk about it. She's a good teacher, she knows what it's like to lose yourself. She's an orphan. Darcy said her family was on vacation in New Mexico when they were in an accident, and only Sister Perpetua lived. Sometimes I picture it on Route 14, the Turquoise Trail. Maybe they're driving a station wagon, and her dad tries to pass this gravel truck on a blind rise. When she tucks her hair back, her one ear looks like melted wax. Sometimes I come up with things she hasn't thought about, and she nods like she's thinking and says we'll talk about it next time.

She treats me nice, her and Mr. Jefferies. Over the years they've never left me, when everyone else did. Only my mom, really. Gainey's still with me. So that's three. If it weren't for them, I don't think I'd be okay now.

So no, I don't know what my IQ is. A hundred something, I guess. I'm not a moron, if that's what you mean. I know what's happening to me.

When they electrocute you, they put this leather helmet on your head. On the top is this bronze knob. It connects to this copper screen inside with a sponge on it. That's the top electrode. They shave your head so it sits right on your skin. The other one's part of the chair; in most states, it's attached to the left leg, sometimes your spine. It's bronze too. They cut the back of your pant leg so it's right against your calf. The straps on the back and the arms they make such a big deal of on TV don't do anything except hold you down.

It's simple. The electricity needs to go from the electrode in the cap to the electrode in the ankle. You're like the piece of wire in a light.

The usual dose is 2000 volts. They do that twice, in some states four times. What's supposed to happen is the current goes through you and stops your heart. What you do is go stiff. All your muscles tense up at once. It doesn't always work like it's supposed to. Back around the turn of the century, one guy went so stiff he ripped the legs off the chair and they had to hold his feet down with concrete blocks. The second jolt made him kick those over. They were going to try a third time, but he'd already died from third-degree burns.

In Florida seven years ago they did this guy named Jesse Tafero; when they threw the switch, flames a foot high shot out of his head. Sparks were flying everywhere. The whole place was filled with smoke. When the guards unstrapped him, his skin fell off his bones like fried chicken. This other guy in Virginia, they got the voltage wrong on him, and the steam built up inside his head until his eyeballs popped and ran down his cheeks. The book I read had all these horror stories. If you made it the chair, you'd be able to use them.

9

I consider myself sane. So does the State of Oklahoma. It's the only thing we agree on.

There's a joke in here, "I'm as sane as the next person." Which over on the Row would be Darcy. She's in for running over her stepdaughter with her car. She didn't just run her over once; she got her caught between the bumper and the garage door and kept ramming her till the door broke. She lived a week. Darcy told me the whole story. Her boyfriend was sleeping with both of them and decided to go with the younger one. You might use that for Natalie and me, I don't know.

When I was first in, I might have been insane. Lamont was gone, Natalie was still in the hospital, and I was coming down after a month of just going. I couldn't think of anything. I'd look at the bolt holding the flange of the bunk on the wall and it would be fascinating, but it didn't mean anything. Nothing did. Everything was made of cardboard. The first time Mr. Jefferies came to see me I could see the wires in his head, the gears that made his mouth go. He wanted to steal my secret numbers so I put my hands over my eyes. I held my breath so I wouldn't hear him. He talked like a recording on the phone; none of the words went together.

"Well," he said, "that's all I've got," and stood up to go.

The guard started to take me away, but he was still looking at me.

"I know what you are," I said. "I saw you in the movie of angels. My dad is watching us on TV. He'll get you."

A few years ago he played that tape for me. I recognized my voice but it wasn't me. Not that that's any excuse.

People say it was all Lamont's fault, that he was the crazy one and we just did what he told us. I don't think that's true. It's easy to think that now. Like I said, it's different when you're there.

When the detectives cleared out our apartment, I asked them to send me any pictures of Lamont they could find. There were a few envelopes from the Motophoto. I sat down on my bunk to look through them, and there we were sitting on the balcony at Mia Casa, kissing Gainey on each cheek. We were so young. There I was in my bikini, posing like a centerfold on the hood of the Roadrunner. There was even a bunch taken at a barbecue in the courtyard with Mrs. Wertz and all our neighbors. It looked like everyone was having a fine time. Even though I knew Natalie had to have taken some of them, Lamont looked happy with me, his arm over my shoulder, his cap pushed back. There was chicken and coleslaw and everyone had a can of beer, but I couldn't remember when they were taken, what day, what the weather was like. The girl in the pictures was skinny, with long hair, and smiled all the time. It was like looking at a good friend, someone who meant a lot to you once but that you hadn't seen in a long time.

How do you tell if you're insane? I still talk to myself. I remember things that never happened and forget ones that did. Some days I pretend I'm cruising Meridian with Lamont and Gainey in his car seat. This is before Natalie, before any of that. We slide into Coney Island and park under the awning and take turns feeding him fries. We both have the chili-cheese foot-long with double onions, and Lamont has to finish mine. Later we roll over to Arcadia Lake and watch the sun set over the water and then go home, and when I'm almost asleep, when I'm lying here with Janille there going through the newspaper, I feel him reach for me. Is that insane?

10

I dream every night. Normal dreams, I think. No more nightmares than anyone else. I don't see the Closes or Victor Nunez or anyone else from the Sonic coming to get me, if that's what you mean. I don't see Lamont or the knives or the fire. I'm not afraid to sleep.

I dream of driving across the desert with a cold grape soda. I dream of sleeping beside Gainey on top of the covers. I dream of being out of here.

It's funny how sometimes your dreams don't change even when your life does. I still dream that the Conoco's going to blow up. I'm working swing, waiting for Mister Fred Fred to relieve me, and this car wobbles in. It's muddy like it just came from the bottom of a lake, and its wheels are falling off. It's just like the beginning of *The Stand*—I'm sure that's where I got it from. The guy behind the wheel is drunk or falling asleep or something, and the car just rolls into the pumps. One of the hoses splits open and the gas pours down on the roof. It's a blue Malibu, the gas washes some of the mud off. In my booth I can see the muffler chugging out exhaust, and the gas streaking down the fender for it. There's no way I can get out from behind the counter. The zodiac scroll dispenser is in the way, and the Slush Puppy machine, all the lighters and Chap Sticks and beef jerky; it's like I'm buried. I look up on the monitor and the Malibu's on fire. The guy's forehead is on the wheel; the horn's going nonstop. There's a sticker by the pump controls that says *In Case of Emergency, Follow Contingency Plan,* but I can't remember what the plan is.

I never get to the end of the dream, to the explosions I know are coming. I started having the dream the week I started working there. It hasn't stopped since. There really was a sticker that said that. It was a joke; the manager never told us what the plan was. It didn't matter. Back then I was too drunk to be any help anyway. I would have stood there and burned.

I dreamed about my dad for a long time after he died. Saturday mornings he'd bring me to the track and let me watch the stable-boys run their workouts. There was hardly anyone else there; you could sit wherever you wanted. In my dream, he was sitting high up in the grandstand and I was climbing the stairs. The stairs had numbers stenciled on them but they weren't in any order. I kept climbing and climbing, and the sun was hot over the grandstand. He was still sitting there with his hat on, far across the rows. And then the PA would come on — not a voice, just this humming — and I knew I was going to fall against the concrete and I'd feel it against my skin forever.

I still have this dream once in a while, but right after he died I had it every night. And others too. There was one where he was driving his Continental around and around the block, and another where he came home from work and gave me all the change in his pockets. He used to do that in real life, but in the dream all the money was from another country; the coins were square and had holes in them and pictures of birds. Once we were talking, and my mom woke me up. I was mad at her all day.

It wasn't just dreams then. Sometimes I'd see him walking down the street. I'd think it was him from the hair, or his hat. Any short, fat man who walked by. It got so I couldn't go to the mall. The gal who helped Natalie write her book made a big deal of this, like it proved I was crazy. Sister Perpetua said it's absolutely normal, so whatever you want to do with it is fine. I loved my dad and I still miss him. He was a regular guy and doesn't have anything to do with what happened.

11

I don't have many fears for myself anymore. My biggest fear is that Gainey won't know who his parents were. That's one reason I'm making this tape. I don't want him reading Natalie's book and thinking it's the truth.

Honey, I love you and I'm always looking over you, and so's your daddy. I know this won't answer everything. We were young and mixed up. Don't you be that way; you see what it leads to.

That's about it for fears. After a while you understand it's a waste of time. There's only so much you control.

I used to be afraid of the weather. Out near Depew you could see it coming a hundred miles away. You were supposed to get hail right before a tornado. It would get dark and then you'd hear it dinging off the hood of our car. My mom loved it. "Look," she said as it hopped in the grass. "How big around would you say those are?" She put a slicker on and a pot on her head and ran outside to put the car in the garage. On the way back she filled her apron, saving the bigger pieces for the freezer. Jody-Jo stayed under the dining-room table, resting his head on the carpet. I turned the TV on to see which counties were getting hit. The weathermen were on all the channels. Pea-sized, they said, marble-sized. Golf ball, baseball, softball. Outside it was like nighttime. My mom went out on the porch.

"Come see the lightning," she said.

I'd only go to the door. Leaves flew in around my shins. The glider was going all by itself; the yard looked like it was covered with mothballs. I knew at work my dad would have to calm the horses down. I was afraid one would kick him in the head like they did in the movies. I was afraid he'd be trying to get home, driving with his windshield wipers on high. He'd have to lie in a ditch when the tornado came. His car could roll over on him, or the wind might pick him up, and then there were the wires still shooting sparks, the poles falling like trees.

In the west, lightning branched down the sky.

"Marjorie, look!" my mom said. "Isn't it beautiful?"

Of all the ways they kill people, the only one I'm afraid of is the firing squad. Here's why. They're made up of five people, usually guards. They stand behind this screen with a slit in it and you sit in a chair with a cloth target over your heart. If they like you, they don't want to be the one to kill you. So what the state does is put a blank in one of the guns. Anyone who's fired a rifle knows a blank doesn't have a recoil like the real thing. It's not like the electric chair, where there's two switches and one's a fake. The same thing goes for lethal injection; there are two buttons that press the plungers. With the firing squad, you know who's doing it.

What happens sometimes is everyone on the squad likes the person, and they all fire away from the heart. It's happened a bunch of times in this country, and even more during war. Everyone hits you in the right side of the chest and you bleed to death while they're reloading. So it's better if they don't like you. When they killed Gary Gilmore, the four shots overlapped at the heart of the target—like a four-leaf clover, the book said. I wouldn't want Janille to have to make that choice.

You asked me about dreams. There's this great dream in Monty Python where this guy's about to be shot. The firing squad's locked and loaded on him, and all of a sudden he wakes up in this chaise lounge in his backyard. His mom's there, and he says, "Oh, Mom, thank heavens, it was all a dream." And his mom says, "No, dear, this is the dream," and he wakes up in front of the firing squad again. That's what it's like sometimes, especially this last week. You expect Darcy to be there but there's only Janille.

The firing squad's not very popular anymore. Only Utah and Idaho use it. It's worse in foreign countries and during wars. They'll shoot you anywhere.

But what about you, what are you afraid of? No one reading your books after you're dead, I bet. Hey, it's okay, they'll still watch your movies, and that's what counts.

12

I don't call myself born-again and I don't go to any particular church. I'm a Christian because I believe in Jesus Christ. That's it and that's all. I don't believe in figuring out all of the world's problems. I don't think I'm going to save anybody, even myself. There's no guarantees of anything.

When I became one is a tougher question. I began reading the Bible my second year here. Even before my trial I was getting letters from people who didn't know me telling me that God had saved me for this. Some of them thought I was innocent and some of them said it didn't matter. It was a kind of tribulation, they said. I would be a witness. I didn't believe them at first because, honestly, some of them sounded crazy. A lot of them talked about the Last Times and the Rapture, things only crazy people would say. I didn't write any of them back and after we lost they stopped writing, all but a few of them.

One day a few months later Janille had a package for me. It had been opened and taped back up like they thought it was a bomb. It was from the Reverend Lynn Walker in Duncan. He'd sent letters before, saying I needed to remember the trials of Job. Now he'd sent me a new Bible, still in its shrink-wrap. He also sent a yellow highlighter with it. His note said I should mark the words that spoke to me, and that I might start with the Psalms. I wasn't forgotten, Reverend Walker said. Every Sunday the congregation of the Duncan House of Prayer was remembering me.

"Got any use for this?" I asked Janille, and stuck it through the bars.

"I already got one," she said, flipping the thin pages. She rubbed her thumb over the gold edges and the rough leather cover like a salesman and handed it back to me. "It's a nice one though."

"Think the library would want it?"

"I think they have enough of them."

"What am I supposed to do with it?" I asked.

And I remember Janille backing away from the bars like it wasn't her problem.

Remember that, Janille—the day my Bible came?

Janille's been a friend. She switched shifts so she could be here tonight. We read a little earlier in Revelations, the seven angels. I haven't told her yet but I want her to have my Bible. Sister Perpetua said that was kind of me, but it's not. Janille knew what I needed then. In a way, she saved me.

I didn't start reading it right then. I put it away where I wouldn't have to look at it. It wasn't for another year that I dug it out again.

It was June because the TV was all repeats and the floors had just started to sweat. The cement turned slick and you had to be careful if you were a pacer. Next door Darcy was listening to her boombox. I had my atlas out, and I was driving through Oak Creek Canyon on Alternate 89, curving along with the water, the red rocks piled high on both sides. Darcy turned her box off, then on again, then off. I rolled out of my bunk and went over to the corner where the bars meet the wall.

"What's up?" I said.

"Your girlfriend Natalie's gettin' out."

"What?" I said, except I didn't say, "What?" Back then I used a lot of unnecessary language. "How?" I said.

"She's done two of her six."

The numbers made sense but it was impossible, like a bill you've forgotten and can't afford to pay.

"When?" I said.

"August first."

I thanked her and went back to my bunk and wondered if I could have Natalie fixed. I couldn't. I didn't have any money, and everyone thought I was crazy. She'd be free and I'd be stuck here the rest of my life.

A little after midnight, I opened the Reverend Lynn Walker's Bible to Psalms and read:

> *Happy is the man*
> *who does not take the wicked for his guide*

nor walk the road that sinners tread
nor take his seat among the scornful;
the law of the Lord is his delight,
the law his meditation night and day.

I uncapped the highlighter and colored the whole thing in.

Sometimes in your books you make fun of religious people. You make them crazy or evil, like in "Children of the Corn" or *Needful Things*. I'd appreciate it if you didn't this once. Just make me the way I am.

13

I was wondering if you'd do a 13. It's like a yellow car's supposed to be unlucky, like our Roadrunner. Lamont said you make your own luck. Maybe he was right.

The worst thing about being executed is the waiting, knowing it's going to happen. Five years ago, when they scheduled that Connie gal, Mr. Jefferies said it was just a matter of time for me.

The last woman they did before that was back in the thirties, this woman who ran a tourist court with her husband out west on Route 66. This was in the Dust Bowl days, when families packed everything in the Model A and headed for California. What this woman and her husband did was let them park in a grove of pecans off behind their cabins. In the middle of the night the man and woman would cut their throats, steal their stake and sell the trucks to a man up in Wichita. They got caught when the man in Wichita stopped buying the trucks. The police found a whole barnful on their property. In the house there were fifty wedding rings on a keychain. They hanged the woman first. Her last words couldn't be repeated.

Then for sixty years, nothing. It was like the rules changed with Connie Whatever-her-name-was. Mr. Jefferies said I was next on the list. There were others who'd been waiting longer, but he said they'd want me because of the publicity. The Marjorie Standiford Case, they called it, like it was all my fault, or the Sonic Killers, like Natalie's book. Not that she made that name up; it was in the papers even before we got caught. She didn't even write the book, it was this lady sportswriter from the *Oklahoman*.

But Mr. Jefferies was straight with me. He said we had somewhere between two to four years. All we could hope was for the governor to lose the election.

"Is he supposed to lose?" I asked, cause I really didn't know. I didn't even know who the governor was for sure.

"We can't worry about that," Mr. Jefferies said. "Right now we need to get this appeal together."

That was five years ago, so I owe him one.

Thank you, Mr. Jefferies. You didn't lose. I should have told you about me and Natalie.

That's the worst thing, the waiting, knowing you can't stall forever. Like I said, I've had two stays, which isn't a lot but it's something. Mr. Jefferies is at his office now, faxing things to the Tenth Circuit Court in Denver, so who knows.

The execution itself only scares me a little. I've read every book in the library on it. They make you lie down on the table and strap you in. Then the technicians stick an IV line into your vein that pumps in a saline solution. They do that for forty-five minutes just to make sure everything's set. A lot of people they do are heavy users, so finding a good vein is a problem. They strap you in and let you lie there like you're going to have an operation, only you're not waiting for a doctor.

There are three chemicals — sodium pentothal's the only one I know. Each one is in a syringe that ties into the IV line. Two people press down buttons in two different rooms, and the machine presses down the plungers in order. One set goes into you, the other drains into a bucket so no one feels bad. First, the pentothal knocks you out, then the machine waits a minute before the next one. The next paralyzes your heart and your lungs. The third just makes sure. They say you choke some but in most cases it's pretty quick. It's not sleep but it's not the gas chamber either. Oklahoma was the first state to switch to it. They used to hang you. You might say something about that.

14

I think me being a woman works both ways. Mr. Jefferies talked with me about this. A man in my position would probably be dead already, but he wouldn't be getting all this bad publicity. People expect killers to be men. A woman's not supposed to kill, and a mother's definitely not. Mr. Jefferies said it was better when we were the Sonic Killers because people tended to blame everything on Lamont, being the man. That's stupid but that's how people think. Since Lamont was dead and we were married, the blame shifted onto me. Even if Natalie didn't lie, she would have gotten off easier because it looked like she was just going along for the ride.

In the beginning I used to get a lot of letters from women's groups, but they all wanted me to say things about Lamont beating me, how that was the reason I stayed with him and why I couldn't see that he was crazy, which isn't at all true. They just wanted someone else to say what they said so people would think it was true.

That's a tough question. Darcy could answer it better than I can. She's read a lot about how terrible it is being a woman. I don't pay that stuff much attention. What's my other choice, being a man? I like men, but I wouldn't trade in a million years. There's a reason they die first.

15

The media doesn't have to satisfy me. They don't even have to tell the truth. All I want from them is equal time.

When Natalie was going to be on "Oprah," I asked Mr. Jefferies if we could do a remote hookup or just something by phone, but Mr. Lonergan said no. I couldn't watch it. Darcy said they played up the same things as always—the fingers, the cop in the desert, Shiprock. They take the weird parts and make them the most important thing, like Natalie's toys.

And they don't even get things right. They called our Roadrunner a Dodge and said that I was a convicted felon. In the *Oklahoman* there was a map of our route west that showed us going through Amarillo instead of around it. Compared to the big things, I guess it's nitpicky of me, but why write it if you're going to get it wrong?

And I'm tired of that picture of me eating the onionburger with the gun in my other hand. I swear it's the only one they use. Someone must think it's funny.

All of that would be fine as long as they didn't drag Gainey into it. They always have to say he was in the car. No matter how small the article is, they get that in.

The whole idea is to make me look stranger so people can pretend they're normal. It's not just me, they do that with everybody. That's their job. No one's interested in how people really are. I mean, it's not interesting that I brought Gainey with us because I couldn't get anyone to sit him and I didn't want to leave him home by himself. It's not interesting that I kept looking out the window to make sure he was okay. They never mention that, they just say he was in the car like I'd forgotten he was there, like the woman who drove away with the baby on the roof.

I never planned on getting out of the Roadrunner. I wasn't supposed to turn it off. I was supposed to wait in the stall until Lamont called me on the intercom, then I'd roll around to the drive-thru and pick up the money. The way it was planned, I would have been with Gainey the whole time. We'd even stopped at the Dairy Kurl up the street and gotten him a junior hot fudge sundae. I was twisted around feeding him when I heard the shots. When we got back to the car, his face was a mess, and I gave Natalie a wet wipe. The whole thing took ten minutes, and except for maybe two minutes in the walk-in fridge, I could see him the whole time. But in the paper they make it sound like I just left him there. I don't care what they say—a mother worries.

I was on TV once when I was a kid. My whole class was. This was right when Skylab was going to crash. Mrs. Milliken, our art teacher, had us make fake space parts out of papier-mâché and put them all over this burnt field behind the school. She called the TV stations and they came out and pretended it had really hit there. My piece was supposed to be the radio, and the news people asked me if they could take my picture with it.

The camera had a light on top of it that blinded me.

"Did you receive any last messages from Skylab before it hit the ground?" the guy with the microphone asked.

"Just one," I said, and screamed as loud as I could.

16

Living on Death Row is like living in a small town. It's slow and everyone knows everyone's business. The population's stable, not like in general, where you have people coming through all the time. There are four of us—me and Darcy on one side, Etta Mae Gaskins and Lucinda Williams on the other.

Etta Mae's next in line after me. She beat an old man in her apartment building to death for his social security check. She was just trying to get him to sign it, she says, but things got out of hand. She hit him with the bar from a towel rack, one of those clear ones. She's a whistler. Any time of day she'll just break into song. You don't notice it after a while and then suddenly you're whistling too. Darcy turns her boombox up so she won't hear her, but I don't mind. She knows lots of old songs you forget, like "The Sunny Side of the Street." Sometimes when I've got my atlas out I pretend they're on the radio and Etta Mae's got this big band behind her and an old-style microphone. Etta Mae's older than the rest of us. She's got high blood pressure so she gets special meals. Once at lunch the trusty with the cart gave me the wrong tray, and I saw what they gave her; it was all boiled, and no Jell-O, no soft drink. I know it's hard on her, because she's always talking about her Aunt Velma's chicken-fried steak and her biscuits and gravy. When we get on food, we can go.

Lucinda is new and hasn't calmed down yet. Last month she scratched Janille's cornea and they took her off to solitary. She shot her boyfriend's wife when she was eight months pregnant, then waited till her boyfriend got home and shot him in the you-know-what. She says she didn't do it. It's a joke around here but you can't laugh.

"Like you innocent, Miss Cut-their-head-off-and-stick-it-in-a-plastic-bag. And you, running over that little girl. You both going to hell, you dumb ugly trash. That's right! And Etta Mae, you gonna hold the door for 'em."

It's funny cause we were all like that at first. She still cries at night. She goes through her cigarettes too quick. She'll learn. Etta Mae'll take care of her.

In general population there's a lot of violence, a lot of people moving through. Someone'll melt the end of a toothbrush and stick a razor blade in it. It's not to kill, they just want to mark the other gal up. There's no respect, no sense of being in this to-gether. Over there, you get a lot of denial—gals saying it was the last deal, the last trick, the last job, they were going to quit right after that, like it was bad luck they got caught. A lot of wouldas and couldas. You don't get that here. Just the amount of time breaks you down, makes you accept things about yourself. It teaches you things you didn't learn outside, like patience and humility and gratitude. It's like religion that way.

We're locked down twenty-three hours a day. The other hour they let us out to use the exercise yard one at a time. We get a shower once every two days. We get three meals. You think you'd look forward to those things but you don't. They just slide by. Lunch always surprises me.

We all do things. Darcy writes poems. Etta Mae paints and makes origami. Lucinda will have to come up with something, otherwise you lose it.

I drive. I open up my atlas and I've got the Roadrunner pegged at 110, headed for the Grand Canyon, the high desert empty on both sides, snow in the ditches. I'm cruising through Albuquerque, the neon of the motels shimmering off the hood. It's like they haven't caught me. No one knows where I am. I swing into the drive-in window of a liquor store and pick up a chilled six of Tecate, slide into a Golden Fried and order the carne adovada burrito for ninety-nine cents. Driving all night, I'm three hundred miles out of Needles and the radio's pulling in Mexico. In six hours I'll be on the Santa Monica pier, the water running in underneath me. At the end, I cut a neat three-pointer and head east again, into the blur of convenience stores and Pig Stands, highway cafes and adobe trading posts. The families of accident victims plant white crosses by the roadside, the names almost too small to read — Maria Felicidad Baca, Jesus Luis Velez. The night burns away and Monument Valley comes up like a cowboy movie, like the sequel to *Thelma & Louise*. The Modern Lovers are on the 8-track and that tach is nailed.

> *Roadrunner, Roadrunner*
> *going fast in miles an hour*
> *gonna drive past the Stop & Shop*
> *with the radio on*

It's been eight years. I've been everywhere.

17

What I'll miss most about the world.

Everything.

My son. I'll miss having fun with him.

I'll miss french fries. I'll miss that first big sip of a cherry slush that freezes your brain and gives you a headache. I'll miss carnivals and amusement parks, state fairs. I'll miss the Gravitron and the Tilt-A-Whirl, the Zipper and the Whip, the Spider and the Roundup, the Roll-O-Plane. I'll miss how your stomach jumps when you go over the top of the Ferris wheel. I'll miss funnel cakes and roasted corn, fried pies and turkey legs, Sno-Kones. I'll miss driving. I'll miss sticking my hand out the window and feeling how heavy the air is.

I already miss a lot. I miss Lamont's belly and how he used to leave a dab of shaving cream behind each ear. I miss our place, our bed—our Roadrunner, obviously.

Weather. Movies.

I don't know, everything. It's a bad question to ask right now. Just say I'll miss living.

18

I feel remorse for my crimes, the ones I did commit, and I feel remorse for the life I was living then. If I could change any one thing, it would be the drinking. That put me on the road to a lot of the other problems.

It's easy to blame other people or circumstances, but I won't. I liked to drink, it's that simple. I liked sitting in the booth at the Conoco and taking a tug of vodka whenever I felt like it. You'd feel it glide warm into you and everything was right. Outside, lights slid by all sparkly when it rained. Inside, all the cigarettes were in rows, all the gum and Life Savers. The heater felt good on your shins, and you'd watch the traffic at the light, everyone in a hurry to get somewhere and the rain coming down, the wipers going. It made you laugh and take another sip. It made you wish your life could just stay that way.

That was the problem—you were always trying to get back there, to that same place. And you were always ready to try. Between Garlyn, Joy and me, one of us always had something going on. We had good times, the three of us, but I look back and wonder if they were worth it. The last time I saw Garlyn she was living in her mother's basement and working at Pancho's Mexican Buffet. We were there for dinner; Gainey was throwing his spoon all over the place and finally spilled his water. She had three stitches in her lip from falling down the cellar stairs. I asked if she was still seeing Danny, because he used to hit her. She was. She said Joy had just gotten fired from the County Line for dumping a platter of hot links on a customer. We laughed because it was just like Joy. That was ten years ago. I don't know what's happened to either of them since.

19

I'd like to say I'm sorry to all the relatives of the Closes, Victor Nunez, Kim Zwillich, Reggie Tyler, Donald . . .

Anderson—Donald Anderson. He was the manager.

I'm sorry, I do remember them, I just can't remember all eight at the same time. Five men and three women, I know that. I'm missing one of each.

What I'd like to say to their families is that I pray for every one of them each and every day. Mr. Jefferies said that Mrs. Nunez wanted to be here tonight. I wanted to invite her, but the state wouldn't let me. I wish she could come. I wish they all could. I'm sure they're outside right now. If that makes the loss of their loved ones easier on them, then fine. In the paper the other day, Mrs. Nunez said she hoped it would be painful, and that I should be killed the same way her son was. I did not kill Victor Nunez. I'd also say that what Natalie did to Kim Zwillich was worse, but I haven't heard her parents complaining in the paper.

Margo Styles. She was the one at the drive-thru window. So there's one more.

What do you say to someone in this situation? I'm sorry isn't good enough. That I'm going to die isn't good enough. I wanted to make a public apology a few years ago, but Mr. Jefferies warned me against it. Forget it, he said, you can't win. All you're going to get for it is grief.

The cop. Sergeant Lloyd Red Deer. He was the reason Mr. Jefferies moved the trial to Oklahoma. New Mexico's still ticked off about that. Mr. Jefferies said that if he weren't a cop, I might have gotten off with life. I'd say I'm sorry to his family and the tribal police, but I don't think it's right that his life counts more than Margo Styles's. When you become a policeman, you understand that the job has some risks and you choose to accept that — like the guy in *Desperation*. Margo Styles didn't have that kind of choice.

I'd say I'm sorry, but what good does that do anybody?

20

To Lamont, I'd like to say I loved you then and I love you still. I don't know why you did what you did, but I forgive you. Jesus forgives you. You will always be the man I love.

I have more but it's private. I'll tell him when I see him.

I'd ask him why. That would be *his* book.

21

How do you tell exactly when you fall in love?

There wasn't any dating like real dating. We were too old for that. We didn't have to play games.

At first we mostly drove around. Cruised the A&W, the Del Rancho, the Lot-A-Burger. We'd buy a cherry limeade and cruise Kickapoo till we got hungry. Listen to tapes.

Lamont's dash was all correct, all the way down to the factory 8-track. We'd go to the Salvation Army or the flea market out at the Sky-Vue and pick up whole boxes of them for nothing, all the classic stuff—Iggy and the Stooges, Blue Cheer, Black Sabbath. When the weather was nice, Lamont would pop the top and turn it up so loud the bass kicked you in the shins. He liked Cream and Jimi Hendrix when we made out. "Little Wing" was our song, the Derek and the Dominos version. Sometimes Lamont would sing along with it, like it was about us. I saw Sting do a cover of it the other day on MTV; it was pretty wimpy.

We'd do stupid things like go bowling or hang out on the seesaw by the Krispy King. We even went fishing once. But mostly we'd cruise.

That 442 was a car. Lamont bought it at the Auto Auction south of town for a thousand dollars and did a full body-off restoration. He loved to talk about what he'd done to that car. He replaced the 400 with a bored-out 455 and swapped the factory tranny for a Muncie rock crusher with a Hurst shifter. He wrote away to Oldsmobile for the original color scheme, he dug through wrecking yards for new seats, he rechromed the bumpers. When he'd see another Cutlass, he'd ask me what year it was, what on it wasn't correct. He liked it that I knew. He was like my dad at that.

The first time Lamont let me drive it I got a ticket. I bet you've got a copy of it. If you don't, you can look it up; it was the Saturday before Thanksgiving, 1984. It was late. We were driving back from Amarillo on I-40. We'd gone to the West Texas Rod and Classic Roundup to look for an exhaust manifold, and his eyes were tired. We'd both done a few black beauties, but he was starting to see things—trails floating like neon over the road. I told him to pull into the next rest area. I could tell he didn't want to, because he knew we'd have a fight.

He hadn't let me drive it yet. It was his baby. Every Sunday he'd wash it by hand, dunking a sponge, then wax it till he could see himself smile in the reflection. Anyone would resent it after a while, but I didn't. He was a kid like that; it was the one thing he owned that made him happy. So I was ready to say it was all right, that we could park in a far spot and try to close our eyes for a little bit.

He pulled in by the dog-walking area but didn't turn the car off.

"Why don't you take over," he said.

He didn't tell me not to do anything, he just got out. We crossed in front of the hood, kissed and got back in.

I was used to a stick from Garlyn's Tercel but I needed to do everything perfect. Lamont put his mirrored shades on and slumped down in the seat. I turned the stereo off so I could hear, jammed the clutch in and searched for reverse. I thought I'd stall, so I fed it some gas and we jerked back.

"Easy there," Lamont said, like Dennis Weaver in "McCloud." It was one of his things.

I rolled through the semis and turned down the long on-ramp. There was almost no first gear, just a few seconds' worth. We reached forty-five in second and blew through the yield sign. Third pressed me into the seat. I laughed and recovered and slammed it into fourth. In the mirror, traffic was dropping back. I was hunched over the wheel, gritting my teeth from the speed.

"How's it feel?" Lamont asked.

"Fast," I said.

"Go ahead, take her up."

I checked the tach and punched it. It was my first time over a hundred. It was like a video game; you had to move over so you didn't run up the backs of the other cars. The wheel shook in my hands; a drop of sweat rolled down my ribs. If we lost a tire, we'd fly across the median and mow down the wedge of oncoming cars like bowling pins. I started giggling.

"Yeah," Lamont said. "That's how it feels."

He reached over and felt me up, and I thought I'd lose it.

"You cold?" he said.

"Just happy," I said.

That's when we passed the trooper.

One Saturday, my dad drove us out Route 66 to Depew. He put a jacket and tie on, and my mom gave him a hard time. He had a pillow to sit on so he could see over the wheel. He pointed things out like we couldn't see them ourselves. There was nothing to see really, just the old house and a few barbecue places on the way — Bob's, the Pioneer, the Rock Cafe. Between them were miles of barbed wire, a few head of cattle, dry creek beds, red dust. On the fence posts hung old tires with NO HUNTING or WILLIAMS FOR SENATE painted on them in white. Behind the weedy tourist courts, the stripper wells nodded like they were tired. It was dumb, but my dad had grown up there. We stopped for a barbecue sandwich about every hour. My dad was loving it. He had his sunglasses on and his elbow out the window, his finger drumming the steering wheel.

> *Now you go through Saint Looey,*
> *Joplin, Missouri,*
> *Oklahoma City is oh so pretty.*
> *You'll see Amarillo,*
> *Gallup, New Mexico,*
> *Flagstaff, Arizona, don't forget Winona,*
> *Kingman, Barstow, San Bernardino.*

"Is this fun or what?" he said, and my mom looked up from her book like he'd said something. She'd grown up there too but didn't seem to care.

I sat in back, waiting for the next stop. At every new place I got another cherry Coke, and by the time we reached Depew, my teeth were gritty and I wanted out of the car. My dad seemed to be driving slow on purpose. My thoughts kept knocking into each other.

"Quit kicking the back of my seat!" my mom said. "And stop bouncing!"

"She's just having fun," my dad said, and started bouncing on his pillow.

My mom used the Lord's name. "Help me," she said. "I'm surrounded by lunatics."

My dad slowed and pulled into our old drive. There was a car there, an ugly old Nomad with Texas plates. Beside the chicken house leaned our old furnace. My father stopped and we all got out. I'm sure there was some wind. My hair was long then and always got in my mouth. Jody-Jo's house was still there, and his chain around the tree, but the glider was gone. There were two bikes on the porch with banana seats and tasseled handgrips.

My dad went up the steps ahead of us and rang the bell, and a minute later a lady came to the door. She was older than my mom, and shorter. In one hand she had a wet paintbrush. She looked at us like we were lost.

"Hello," my father said, and while he was explaining everything, a man in an OSU sweatshirt came to the door. He opened the screen to shake my father's hand.

"Terry Close," he said, and everyone said hello.

"And this is our Marjorie," my father said.

When Mrs. Close shook my hand, the paint left a white streak on my palm.

They had two girls about my age, I forget their names. They said hi and disappeared up the stairs.

Now there's something you could do—like in *The Dead Zone* or *The Drawing of the Three*. I could touch Mrs. Close's hand and see her in the trash bag. Would that be neat? Or Natalie in the living room, or the fire.

At the time, all I saw was their furniture covered with drop cloths and the bare bulbs of the lamps. The fresh paint made me sneeze.

Mr. Close was sorry we'd come all that way, but they had to get the room done. He wished they weren't so busy. It was nice of us to drop by. Maybe we could get together sometime.

"You can bet on it," my dad said.

"Fantastic," Mr. Close said. "Hope to see you again soon."

22

The first time I had sex I threw up.

This was at the Sky-Vue Drive-In, in the bed of Monty Hunt's Ford Ranger. We were watching *Halloween* and drinking pink Champale. We'd been going out all summer, and I was going to be a junior, so I thought it was time. We'd been close before. I'd made him beg me.

I heard it hurt, so I was two bottles ahead of Monty. He had the truck backed up on the hump with the speaker hanging over the side. It was warm but the bugs were bad, and we were under a blanket. We were kissing, getting our faces wet. I was wearing anklets with little pom-poms in the back, that was all. I'd started the night with shorts and a tube top but they were gone. In my bag I had another pair of underwear.

I opened my legs and let Monty put his hand there. I think I surprised him. He dug around down there, then got on top of me; the movie was blue on his face. The music was building up to a killing. Two speakers over sat a family in lawn chairs, eating popcorn out of a giant yellow bag.

He couldn't find his way in at first, and I had to help him. It's funny how they want it so much and then don't know what to do. I could barely feel it in me. He had his mouth open and I could see up his nose. It felt uncomfortable, almost like the beginning of cramps, and then something gave way, like when you realize you have a nosebleed. It stung, and I tipped my chin up so he couldn't see that it hurt me. The Champale wasn't working. He was pushing against my stomach; I felt like I had to go to the bathroom. Above me, upside down, Jamie Lee Curtis was riding through a graveyard with this other girl, getting stoned. Monty stopped all of a sudden and let out a hot breath right in my face and fell on top of me like he'd been stabbed. His back was sweaty, and I could feel him seeping inside me. We didn't use anything, and I knew I was going to get pregnant.

"I love you," he said, still gasping. He didn't even say my name.

And what was I supposed to say? That I felt sick, that I wished I hadn't let him?

I said it back.

"Are you okay?" he said.

I knew there would be blood but not so much. I wiped my thighs with the blanket and folded it over.

"I'm okay," I said. "I just need to clean up."

"I've got Kleenex," he said, and reached through the back window of the cab and handed me the box. He knelt there staring at me.

"Watch the movie," I said.

I stuffed some up there, but I still felt sick, so I put on my top and my old underwear and my shorts and found my clogs. Monty wouldn't leave me alone. "I'm okay," I kept telling him. "I just need to use the bathroom." He wanted to come with me, but I finally shouted at him, and he let me go.

I jumped down from the tailgate and almost fell. My legs were shaky and my stomach was churning like a washing machine. Everything down there stung. I stumbled over the dusty mounds toward the red fluorescents outlining the snack bar. It was circular and shaped like a witch's hat, the projector in the top part. You could see the movie scissoring through the air. We were in the back, like a mile away. The last hundred feet were deserted. A green light burned on each unused speaker like an eye. Halfway there, I knew I wasn't going to make it. I stopped and leaned against a speaker pole and heaved up everything I'd eaten—the Champale and the mustard fries, the nachos and Dots—all of it splashing hot over my Dr. Scholl's. I spit to clean my mouth and kicked dust over everything and went on.

My thighs were sticky, and getting sick had made me cry, so my face was a mess. I knew the bathrooms were by the front, so I walked around the outside and slipped in, hoping no one would see me.

Inside there was a line—seven or eight girls smoking, hands on hips. I stood outside in the pink glow, the movie huge behind me. The music was building again. A fat guy carrying a little kid in pajamas on his shoulders was coming. I pretended to be looking for something I'd dropped, then when he was even with me, I fell in beside him. The girls inside didn't even look. I walked straight past them and into the men's room.

There was one guy at a urinal, but he didn't turn around. I wetted a handful of paper towels and took them to the farthest stall and locked the door. It was so filthy I didn't sit down. I threw the Kleenex in the toilet and the water went red.

As I was wiping my legs, I heard the guy getting some paper towels and then the door closing.

In the mirror I looked the same, maybe a little buzzed, a little tired, but the same girl I'd been before. I didn't think I'd learned anything.

Outside, the girls in line took one look at me and ran for the men's room.

Monty was waiting back at the truck, asking the same questions.

"I'm fine," I said, and let him hold me. Now that I look back on it, he was being as sweet as he knew how, but right then I hated him.

"Marjorie," he said, real serious, like he was going to follow it with something big like "I love you" or "I want to marry you."

I didn't give him the chance.

"Hey," I said, "did you leave me any of that Champale?"

That was a weird time for me, fifteen and sixteen. I think it is for most girls. The world can be so perfect, and then it can just suck. That's unnecessary language, but I've already said it; just don't have me say it in the book. People are mean or dishonest for no reason. It makes you angry, and angry with yourself for being that way sometimes.

I was weird, I know that now. I think my mom blames it on my dad dying right in front of me, but I don't think that's it. Natalie's book tries to say that. That's some of it maybe, but not all. Don't make too big a deal of it.

I read somewhere that your dad left early, so you know how people try to pin everything on that. You know not to fall for it.

The big thing when I was fifteen is that I got a job and started drinking a lot of diet Pepsi. I was a fry man at Long John Silver's. That's what they called me—a fry man. I worked the Fry-o-lator. Actually they call them fryes there. Some other goofy stuff they had were chicken planks and hush puppies and corn cobbettes, which were just frozen ears of corn snapped in half. You had to wear these ugly blue uniforms with this dorky bow at your throat; they were made of polyester and stuck to your sweat. It was boring because no one ever came in besides the dinner rush. When an order did come in, the girl at the counter said it into her microphone, and I tossed a breaded fish square into the grease. You had to jump back fast or it would get your hands. I'd fill up the metal basket with frozen fryes and lower it into the grease. Everything there was frozen. We used to play broom hockey with the filets; they hurt when they hit your shins.

I wasn't really drinking then, not like every day. I'd come in after school, and the first thing I'd do is pour myself a jumbo diet Coke. The biggest cup they had then was 44 ounces, now it's 64. I'd drink two of those before the dinner rush and I'd be flying.

In some ways it wasn't a bad job, compared to some of the ones I've had. You didn't have to do much. The manager's name was Cissy, and when there was nothing to do, she made us sweep. You'd sit down to read a magazine or something—maybe I could be reading *The Stand*, the original one, because it was about that time. If Cissy saw you sitting down, she'd get on the microphone and say, "Grab a broom." We'd go to the bathroom to read so much that she set a time limit on how long you could be in there. She'd come in and knock on your stall.

I liked the longer version of *The Stand*. I liked the original one too. Even the miniseries was good, with the guy from *Forrest Gump* with no legs. I thought his dog was great. It's such a great story. Do you think someday you'll put out an even longer version? You could just keep adding to it. I'd read it.

You could do the same thing with all your books, the ones people like. Not like *It* or *The Eyes of the Dragon* or *The Tommyknockers*, but the good ones. I could read a lot more of *'Salem's Lot*.

Anyway, it wasn't a bad job. I could quit anytime cause I was still living with my mom. I didn't really need the money for anything. Monty always paid for everything.

One night when we were out on a date, Monty took me to Charcoal Oven. It's this old-time drive-in off Northwest Expressway with this great neon, this chef guy in a hat in six different colors. You could see it for miles. We pulled up and ordered, and Monty said to me, "What do you want to drink?"

And automatically I said, "Large diet Coke."

So he goes, "Large diet Coke," to the speaker.

"Diet Pepsi okay?" the girl on the speaker says.

Monty looks at me like it might not be okay. He was like that, he wanted everything to be just right. I think he was scared that he wasn't.

"Whatever," I said.

So we cruised around to the window and Monty paid and we picked a stall and backed in so we could look at the neon. We sat there picking the pickles out of our hickory burgers and squeezing the ketchup packets onto napkins, trying not to make a mess. Monty was always worried about his carpet. He had cup holders that attached to the lip of the window, and I stuck my diet Pepsi in mine.

The first sip I took was weird because I'd been drinking diet Coke so long. The diet Pepsi was sweeter and heavier and not as fizzy. I didn't like it at first. I must have made a face because Monty was like, "We can go around and order something else."

"It's okay," I said, not because it was, but because I was tired of him asking me. I was tired of him calling us "we." He was the wrong one, and I'd given myself to him and now I couldn't get it back. He was nice, he was fine, but I hated myself and I hated him. I hated "we." It was just bad.

So we sat there eating our hickory burgers and curly fries, watching the neon build the man in the chef's hat one piece at a time, and little by little I felt the caffeine creeping through me, except it wasn't like the diet Coke, it didn't build to a level and spread. It just kept going. My heart was jumping so much I had to catch my breath, and a chill made me hard in my bra. It was better than anything Monty had ever done for me.

When we were done, I asked him to pull around and order another.

The next morning I woke up with a huge headache, but I was

used to that. Before homeroom I bought a diet Pepsi from a machine and I was fine.

I only lasted another two weeks at Long John Silver's. At break I'd walk across the parking lot to the Western Sizzlin' and buy a large diet Pepsi with no ice. Two, three times a night. It didn't make sense. That's when I applied at Sonic.

Everyone thinks it's funny that I worked there. Don't make it funny, please. It's a cheap joke and not fair.

Leo's has Pepsi. You'd be amazed how few places do. McDonald's, Burger King, Wendy's—that's all Coke. Burger King used to be Pepsi but they changed. They must have gotten a better deal or something. Sonic's interesting because it's half and half; it's up to the owner. Which do you like better?

I've never had Jolt, but Darcy says it's amazing. I would have ordered it if I could.

23

Lamont and I first made love on October 27th, 1984. This is later that same night he drove me home for the first time.

I don't remember us talking much in the car, just hello stuff, what's your name, what do you do. He was working at the Wreck Room, this collision shop over on Reno. He didn't say if he had his own place—and he could have, you know? He was nice that way. At one point he asked if I'd had a little to drink, and we joked about my job.

"I've been coming in every night for two weeks now," he said. "I thought you might notice. That's why I drove off earlier."

"I noticed," I said.

He was punching it between the lights. You could feel that 455 through the seats. It was like riding a motorcycle. Around ninety, the car seemed to grow lighter, to rise up on the frame like we might take off.

I used some unnecessary language like I used to. "It's some nice machine."

"It's all right. What I really want is a Super Bird."

"With that ugly old spoiler?" I said. "Too expensive. What's wrong with a regular old Roadrunner?"

"That or a GTX."

"How 'bout a Super Bee?"

"Same difference," he said.

"You know it's not," I said.

He said my name then. He might have said it before but this is the first time I heard it.

"Marjorie," he said, "what kind of car did your daddy drive?"

"My *mom* used to drive a Toronado," I said. "Now she drives a boat-tail Riviera. My dad drove a Continental."

"There's a good-sized car," he said, like I'd passed a test, and I knew I had him. I could do anything with him I wanted to.

He was going to drop me off, but Garlyn and Joy weren't home yet, so I invited him in. The dishes were like an earthquake around the sink. I set my purse on the kitchen table. The pint was right in the box of peas where I'd left it. I reached in to get it, and he held me from behind. The freezer let off steam. His hands ran up my front. The bottle stuck to my fingers.

"We don't need that," he said.

"It's not for we," I said, and broke the seal on it. I tipped it up and he kissed me on the throat. "You want some?" I said, and when he didn't look, I knocked the heel of it soft against his temple.

He opened his eyes, then shook his head and kept going down.

"More for me," I said, and took a sweet, hot swig.

He picked me up with his arms around the backs of my thighs. I slapped the freezer shut before he carried me out of the room.

"Where are we going?" I said.

"How 'bout right here?" he said by the couch.

"Nope," I said.

I made him carry me around until he found my room.

I turned on the smallest light. It was almost Halloween, and Garlyn had bought candy. On the floor beside my mattress was a mess of Reese's Cup wrappers and empty Pixie Sticks. The closet door was propped open by a pile of dirty clothes. I turned the light off and pushed him onto my bed and took a slug before joining him.

We were in the middle of it when I heard the back door close. I'd forgotten that Joy and Garlyn would be getting home. I was on top, still sipping that last precious inch. I couldn't reach the door to close it, so I said, "Hang on," and popped off him.

"No," he said, and when I got back he was useless. The air was cold on me. We both said some unnecessary things.

We didn't go anywhere though. Garlyn and Joy were banging around the kitchen, trying to make something. We just started talking. It wasn't uncomfortable. I had a stash of Reese's cups keeping cold on the windowsill, and we laid there eating them, holding hands and watching the headlights cross the wall. I had a picture of my dad in the winner's circle with Unlikely Guide, a big blanket of roses over him. Lamont got up out of bed and looked at it. The headlights made his back white as a statue, his skinny hips.

"Come here," I said.

He turned to me and pointed at the picture. "Is this him?"

"Yeah," I said. "Now come here."

And that was the real first time. It wasn't great, it was only okay, but it meant something. I could tell it meant something, and back then not much did.

24

My sexual fantasies. Do you mean now or back then?

Now it would be having Lamont again, just for a night together, to hold him against me. That's the worst thing about the Row, you never touch anyone. In general population there's some relief. It's cruel and unusual, Darcy says.

I guess I'd have him every way I could and in between we'd talk. We'd sleep. He was nice and warm in bed. If you were freezing, all he'd have to do was get in and you'd warm right up. It was just his metabolism. In the middle of the night, he'd have to throw the blankets off his side, and in the summer, forget it.

Or driving, we were always happy driving. We'd be flying down the interstate and all of a sudden he'd pull off. Not into a rest area, just by the side of the road, and we'd climb into the backseat. When the semis came by, the whole car would shake.

But the best was on speed. Your whole skin was just ready. And Lamont knew that. He'd take his time, going lightly over all of me. The shivers would just rip through you. That's probably it, the one I'd choose. Make it take forever.

Those aren't really fantasies, but I don't have anything else. All that whipped cream and leather stuff seems silly to me.

There were a few things Lamont's old girlfriend Alison wouldn't do that I would. I liked doing them for him. He was always grateful, and always kind. We had a rule—everything was okay as long as no one got hurt.

Lamont liked lingerie—the black satin bras with holes cut in them, the garters. I was happy to wear stuff like that for him but it never did anything for me. Later I cut all of that stuff up right in front of him. But I'm sure we'll get into that later.

Once I rented hip boots for a costume party, the kind with spike heels. I was going as Vampirella, remember her? He liked them so much that I never took them back. I'd surprise him with them sometimes. I'd pretend like I was getting up to go to the bathroom and come back with them on.

But for me, I guess I don't get too excited about that stuff anymore, not after Natalie. It's fun but it's not what you really need. In here, you think about that—what you need and what you can do without. You can do without a lot of things. Fantasies might be one of them.

When I was a kid, I used to have fantasies about sex, but not like fantasies fantasies, more like guesses at what sex was.

I once saw my mom and dad having sex. It was a Saturday and it was raining, so my dad didn't have to go in to the track. I didn't know that. All I knew is that I wanted someone to put my cartoons on. I had my bunny and my blanky, all I needed was the TV on, so I went into their room to ask.

My mom's wrists were tied to the bedposts with belts, and her ankles, and there was a pillowcase over her head with holes for her eyes and mouth. My dad was standing above her on the bed. He had a belt on, and something metal on his thing. He balanced a hand on the wall, lifted one foot and stuck his big toe in her mouth.

"Tell me you like it," he said, and she tried to, but just grunted.

"Tell me you want it," he said, and she grunted.

"Where do you want it?"

She jerked and struggled against the belts, lifting herself off the bed.

"No," he said. "Not yet."

He knelt on her shoulders, and I couldn't see her head anymore. I went into the living room and sat on the couch across from the TV.

"Hey, pumpkin!" my dad said later, when he came out in his bathrobe. "Why didn't you come get us?"

I used to wonder if every boy had a metal thing on his thing, and if I'd have to wear a pillowcase. In the bathtub, I scrubbed my toes good, and sometimes late at night I'd bend my foot up to my mouth, cover my eyes with my pillow and take a guilty lick. I decided it was like the sip of beer my father offered me at dinner. There was no reason to worry about it. Right now it made me sick but when I was older I'd probably get to like it.

And it was true, you know. I did.

25

I moved in with Lamont on November 15th, 1984. Garlyn and Joy helped us move my stuff. They were sorry to see me go but glad to have the room back. They said they wouldn't tell my mom or Rico where I was. I cried a little; I'm not good at saying goodbye.

Lamont's place was in a complex off East Edwards where there were a lot of college students—Casa Mia. It was loud, but you could get anything you wanted any time of night. Lamont had his own parking spot. Every night he stretched a cover over the 442.

It was a one-bedroom with a big living room and a kitchenette, a balcony with dusty lawn chairs on it. The bathroom was too small for two people, but we got along. He had a big TV and a VCR, and every night when we got home we'd watch a movie and have fun on the couch. He loved *Sugarland Express*, and *Badlands*, and he loved Paul Newman in *Winning*. *The Blues Brothers*, *Dirty Mary Crazy Larry*—all the great car movies. He even taped episodes of "Route 66." I knew them all from when I was a kid. It was great.

Describe it. I don't know what you want. The walls were off-white, that spray-stucco stuff. Off-white wall-to-wall carpet. Fake wood cabinets in the kitchen. A dishwasher that never worked.

The balcony had a view of the old elementary school parking lot; that was always busy.

Not a lot of furniture. A gold crushed-velvet couch and two matching chairs. His water bed and dresser were a matching set too, in dark wood. The water bed had these drawers underneath but they weren't really big enough for anything. It had a mirror in the headboard we both liked.

No plants. Nothing on the walls. His old girlfriend Alison had taken all of that stuff and he'd never replaced it. There were still nails in the walls. In the bathroom he had a J. C. Whitney catalogue. *The Home of Chrome*, the cover said, and inside he'd circled everything he wanted—valve covers and traction bars, Hooker headers. The sink leaked, you could hear it in the middle of the night. Someone had stuck a Budweiser label to the corner of the mirror, and someone else had peeled half of it off.

Our buzzer was always broken and one night the door of our mailbox was kicked in. The vestibule was full of leaves and red dust, and the sod on the lawn was dead. A sign by the sidewalk said efficiencies were available.

What I remember most about it though is the two of us eating dinner in, or wasting the morning reading the paper. Just us lying on the carpet, the whole place quiet, just the air conditioner going. Casa Mia had great air conditioning.

The quiet during the day, that was the best thing. Sometimes we'd stop reading and look up at each other. In the first week we made love in every room in that place, even the kitchenette.

26

Not much. We ate out a lot, just because of where we worked, and what hours.

Diet Pepsi in cans, for the car, and in the two-liter bottle for there. Oranges for vitamin C. Cold cuts, usually hard salami and provolone cheese. Wheat bread.

Later when Lamont was dealing, he kept everything in the freezer. I showed him how to turn a Ben & Jerry's carton into a safe. You take a full one and run hot water around it and the ice cream comes out like a plug. Then you cut the bottom half off. You take one of those little I Can't Believe It's Not Butter tubs, put your stash in it and put the ice cream on top of it. When we'd get an ounce, we'd buy two or three flavors.

The usual stuff in the door, ketchup and stuff, tartar sauce. A gallon jar of pickle chips I'd steal from the Village Inn when I worked there. When I was at the Catfish Cabin I'd steal boxes of their steak fries. Sometimes we'd eat them when we watched our movies. On the side of the box it said *Large French Fries*, and Lamont would always say, "I'm about ready for some Large French Fries, how about you?"

Eggs, bacon, butter. Milk. Frozen juice. Pink lemonade in the summer.

Beer. Lamont loved his beer. Miller High Life. Not Lite and not Bud, and forget about Coors. We wouldn't even go to Mazzio's Pizza because they didn't have Miller. We'd get a suitcase every Thursday.

Actually we ate more stuff out of the cupboard. Tuna fish, chicken noodle soup. Cereal, lots of cereal. Lamont had a thing for Cap'n Crunch. No crunchberries though.

I had to clean it even though it was his. I put in a box of Arm & Hammer every month or two. You forget them and they turn into a brick.

I hope that's enough. It's a weird question. Why do you have to know that anyway?

27

A typical day back then.

We were both on swing, so we'd sleep in. We'd get up around ten, get showered, get dressed. I'd make breakfast and Lamont would go down and get the paper. He liked strawberries cut up on his Cap'n Crunch. We'd listen to the radio while we ate, then lounge around in the living room, moving around the rug with the sun. He liked to look at the classifieds.

This was right when he was getting ready to sell the 442 and buy the Roadrunner. The 442 reminded him of Alison, so it started reminding me of Alison, and it had to go. He was almost done with it, he just had a little detailing to do. He was going to use the money to buy five pounds of sinsemilla he could sell in half pounds around the college. That way he could restore the Roadrunner and still have some money in the bank.

He'd read the classics and sports cars to me.

"Fairlane," he'd say, "Falcon, Goat, Goat, Goat."

"Come on," I said, "cut to the Mopar stuff."

For a while it looked like we might buy a Hemi 'Cuda, but

when we went to test it, the wheel wells were full of Bondo. They said it was a Texas car.

"Texas, Maine maybe," Lamont said.

We went back to the classifieds.

"Who wants a Mustang," he'd say, "or a Vette. That's a car for someone with no imagination."

"You want that little Rambler Scrambler," I said.

"There you go," he'd say. " '70 AMX."

We'd do that until lunch, then we'd make sandwiches or go out to Chloe's Onion Fried or Taco Tico or Smoklahoma. Sonic was always good. Lamont always knew when I didn't want to cook.

After lunch we'd do all the little things we had to do. Go to the laundromat, food-shop, get gas. You could show us at the post office, it was right about that time. I was trying to stop drinking so much, and Lamont wanted to go everywhere with me, just to make sure. He'd drop me off at the Conoco and come in to make sure I punched in. I didn't like it at first, but after a while it was nice.

I paid Ronny the day guy to buy me a pint every day. He'd leave it under a Bazooka bubble gum bucket under the counter. I remember one day he was sick and I looked under the bucket and it wasn't there. And there's nothing you can do then, you just sit there in the booth and wait it out.

I'd drink the pint like I was drinking a quart and I'd be done by seven and feeling pretty good. Then I'd call across the street to China Express or the Red Barn and someone would run something over. El Chico was over there too, but their dinner rush was too crazy to spare anyone. My favorite was the Barnbuster. After a pint, I just loved saying, "I'll have a Barnbuster, please." A lot of things are funnier over the phone when you're drunk.

After I ate I'd straighten up. We sold a lot of milk at night. I

Windexed the doors. I'd go through a hardpack of Marbs and a valu-pak of Care Free peppermint before Mister Fred Fred showed up. I told you he'd come back, didn't I? This isn't the real place he comes back, but still.

He didn't have a car, Mister Fred Fred. He'd just come walking across Broadway with his notebook like My Favorite Martian or someone. He was always early because he wore two watches, one on each arm. They were the exact same, like he'd gotten a deal on them. At first I thought maybe one was five minutes fast and the other was ten, or they were an hour behind each other, or the time on Mister Fred Fred's planet. When I finally looked at them, they didn't have anywhere near the right time. They were just way off. I didn't even ask.

He'd come in and we'd do the drawers and right on time Lamont would pull up and open the door for me. I never had to wait.

When he kissed me, I knew he was checking my breath. We'd talk about our day, anything funny we'd seen. If it was summer or it was nice, we'd go home and get cleaned up and cruise Broadway. We'd get in the shower together, and sometimes we'd just forget about cruising. I didn't mind one way or the other. It was nice to be out with Lamont; I was proud he was mine. I liked people looking at us.

His friends hung out down around the Kettle or up by Daylight Doughnuts. I didn't know many of them, I just knew their rides. They were pretty straight, just regular gearheads. The guy to beat was this guy named Paul with a black '68 Charger R/T with a 440. Heavy car, all steel except the hood. Guys would come up from the city to try him. We'd all go out to Memorial, the last half mile east where it's the access road beside the Kirkpatrick Turnpike. Only one guy came close, this guy from Moore with a '70 Buick GS; he got the jump off the line but Paul ran him down. He had a nitrous kit, and on Saturdays he'd take it out to the strip and run low 10s with it, then Monday he'd drive it to work. It was quick and legal too. I think that's what finally convinced Lamont to go with the Roadrunner.

We cruised and maybe ate some cottage fries at the Kettle and then went home and got stoned and watched TV. Fooled around. Around two we'd move into the bedroom and get ready for bed. Brush our teeth, that stuff. Lamont used Listerine. He was terrified of the dentist. You had to swish it thirty seconds for it to do any good, and when you spit it out the whole bathroom smelled. I used to tease him about it.

I set the alarm and got into bed first, and then he'd stand there wearing nothing and blow his nose. That was the last thing he did before he turned out the light. I'd hold the covers open for him to get in. He was always warm, even his hands.

"Marjorie," he'd say. "Marjorita."

"What?" I'd say.

"You know what I love about you?"

"No."

"Everything," he'd say.

We'd talk after, and then he'd sleep, but something about it made me awake. I'd lie there listening to him breathe, watching his face change in his dreams. I was afraid it was love. I didn't know what to do if it was. It had never happened to me before. It never really has since.

That was back then, in the beginning. All of that changed when Natalie came.

28

Happy. Yeah, we were very happy. We knew it too. It was probably the best time of my life.

What?

Hang on, it's Janille again. It might be dinner.

Sure, bring it in.

I'm just kidding, I know the rules. You're so wired tonight. Did they remember the brisket this time?

Whoa, that's a lot. Okay, let me get this.

Sorry. I'm going to turn you off while I eat, if that's all right. I don't want to make a mess of the recorder. It's almost time to flip the tape anyway. I'll talk to you later.

SIDE B

CHECK, CHECK

Okay, I'm back. You missed some serious barbecue, I'm telling you. And I didn't even have to pay for it. That's Leo's, the original over on 36th and Kelley, the real one. When you come out to do your research you should get Mr. Jefferies to take you. It's great. The oven has these big steel doors. When they open them to get your order, the smoke rolls right into the room and just sits there under the ceiling tiles. It smells like the whole place is on fire. The key is lots of black pepper and vinegar. I know you're from Maine, so you'll probably want the regular sauce, not the hot. Get a pound of everything except the barbecued baloney; that's for tourists. And don't forget the strawberry-banana cake. It doesn't look like much but it's perfect to cool your mouth down after. Diet Pepsi only does so much.

You know how when you're really stuffed you say you're never going to eat again? This time it's true.

Sorry, I'm a little tired right now. Big food always makes me sleepy. I did Darcy's white crosses with my diet Pepsi, so I'll be fine in a little bit. I should get going on your questions. It's already nine because "Primetime" is on; Janille never misses it.

I was wondering though, even if it is a novel, if you say Natalie did it, can she sue you? What about Gainey's money, could she get any of that? I guess I should've asked Mr. Jefferies all this before we signed the contract. Too late now, huh?

That's all right, it doesn't change what I'm going to say. You paid your money so you're getting the whole story, like it or not. What you do with it after that is up to you. You're the big writer.

29

I don't remember exactly when I first did speed with Lamont. We didn't start shooting it right away. That wasn't for a long time. First we just did pills.

Weekends we'd go to car shows out of town, over to Albuquerque or down to Houston. We needed the 442 to win some prizes so we could sell it for more. We always took a few black beauties to help us get back. Lamont got them from this Indian guy in our complex who worked for the college. India Indian. They were mostly caffeine, I think, because that summer when the guy wasn't around, Lamont got some from Paul with the Charger, and they were different.

We were going to Phoenix, about six of us, all in different categories. There was a guy named Cream with a tubbed Mach I and someone with a Yenko Nova. It would take about 16 hours, taking our time. Everyone except us had a trailer. They all left Thursday morning. Lamont figured we could do it in one shot, 40 all the way across and then 17 down. We'd leave after work around midnight and get in around dinner on Friday; that way we'd still have time to clean up the car before the prelim judging Saturday morning.

Thursday before work, Lamont packed up his buffer and the sheepskin mitt he used to do the hood. He packed up his creams and waxes and the mirror squares that went under the engine and the rear end. I picked out a case of 8-tracks and made some sandwiches we wouldn't eat.

Work took forever. I'd almost stopped drinking by then, and I was proud of myself for saving my pint for Monday. Lamont was early. I had my drawer closed out before Mister Fred Fred made it across the street.

I can take that drive now, mile by mile. 40 West. It's what they built to replace that stretch of Route 66. It's just like the song:

> *You'll see Amarillo,*
> *Gallup, New Mexico,*
> *Flagstaff, Arizona, don't forget Winona—*

Actually Winona's before Flagstaff, that's why he says don't forget it. But that part of 40 is what we were on. My dad said it took them five interstates to replace Route 66 and none of them were half as fun.

I don't know. The Cadillac Ranch is something, and that's on 40. It's right past Amarillo, in the middle of a field, a line of Caddys sticking up out of the ground like Stonehenge. We went through there around four in the morning on our way out and didn't see it, but we stopped on the way back and walked out to see them. We were happy because we'd won our bracket; Lamont had the check in his wallet and his back pocket buttoned up. We were both flying, and the sun hurt our eyes. It was early morning; there was no one else around and just a little wind. The field had alfalfa in it and dried cow pies. There was a path all the way out. In the distance you could see a silver water tower like a rocket. The Caddys were half buried and spray-painted red. We walked around them, stupid from being in the car so long. There was graffiti all over them, and broken beer bottles in the dust.

"They're in order," Lamont said, and pointed out the tail fins. "There's one for every different fin." He named and dated them and gave me their whole histories. Biarritz, Coupe de Ville, Fleetwood, Calais.

"They look like bombs that haven't gone off yet," I said. "They look like graves. Look how the water sits inside the taillights. And how come there's no seats—did people steal them?"

We'd been talking nonstop since the drugs kicked in, but I felt like there was a lot more to say. All the words in my head were going by like traffic. When I stopped talking, my thoughts ran out ahead of me. We stood there holding hands, looking at it like a monument for the dead or something.

"Hey," Lamont said, like he was going to say something important, "is this some speed or what?"

"Tell me about it," I said. "Can I drive now?"

"No tickets," he warned me.

"Hey," I said, "we're rich."

Back on the highway, Lamont cracked a diet Pepsi for me and stuck it in the cup holder. It didn't taste like anything. He slid a hand through one leg of my shorts. It was hard to concentrate on him and keep my eyes on the road. I kept speeding up and then letting my foot off the gas. Finally we pulled over. The air conditioning was chilly. The semis made the whole car shake.

"We should do this every day," I said.

Later we stopped at a Speed-A-Way and Lamont bought a copy of that month's *Old Car Trader*. He went right to the Chrysler-Plymouth-Dodge section and started flashing me pictures of Roadrunners. He read off a bunch of them that had been completely restored.

"We can't afford that," I said, like he didn't know.

"Here you go," he said. "1969, documented Hemi, 4 speed, lemon twist yellow, 84 K miles, good condition, no rust, must sacrifice at 7500."

"Where is it?" I said.

He looked up the area code on a chart in the front.

"Wichita."

"What time is it?" I said.

"Nine thirty-five."

"How much cash you got on you?"

"I've got the checkbook," Lamont said.

And that's how we got The Sonic Killers' Death Car.

There's an exhibit, you know, right outside of Tucumcari. I saw a picture in this book on roadside attractions. They've got one of Liberace's Rolls-Royces and the original Monkeemobile, even a *Christine*. Right in the middle of them is our Roadrunner with a Sonic tray on the window and a plastic hamburger and fries. You can even get a postcard of it. It looked good, and I thought Lamont would have liked that, knowing someone was taking care of his baby. Sometimes when I'm driving, I'll pull up outside and wait for someone to recognize me. Then I just scream right out of there.

I haven't said anything about Lamont's folks because they weren't really part of our life. The Gants were his fifth set of foster parents, and he'd only been with them a few months before he turned legal and got a place of his own. Nothing against them, they just weren't around that much. After Gainey was born we went over to see them one Sunday. They lived off Wilshire in a so-so neighborhood and they had three other foster kids by then. We got dressed up to go over, and while we were there everything was fine, but when we got home Lamont got all quiet. I put Gainey down for the night. Lamont was on the couch, still in his good clothes but with his tie undone.

"They're busy," I said.

"I know," he said. "They were fine."

"Want a beer?" I said, and he said, "Sure," but like it wouldn't help. That was the last time we saw them. They didn't come to my trial.

His real mother sold Lamont for a car when he was a baby, or that was the story. His father wasn't her husband. The car broke down and his mother went to ask for him back and got in a fight with the other woman. They got arrested and the court took Lamont away. It was a big story in the newspaper back then.

That's about the only story Lamont tells. He says it was a '51 Mercury Monterey, and that's why he'd never buy a Mercury even though he loves the old Cyclones. The other three families he wouldn't talk about, or how he got the scar on his neck.

I'm telling you this because I don't think you should just blame the drugs, like in *Reefer Madness*. I don't mean you should blame Lamont's being a foster kid either, I just think the reader should know that. He was very proud of being a father to Gainey; it wasn't something he took for granted.

30

Crank, meth, crystal. White. Lamont used to say, "If it ain't white, it ain't right." That was the good stuff. I've heard of kids making bathtub crank from muriatic acid and Vicks inhalers. It's all junk really, the worst thing in the world for you.

The pills you'd get were bennies or black beauties, christmas trees, purple hearts. Most of them were caffeine. They made your gums sweat so bad you had to spit all the time.

We just called it crank, or speed, or drugs. It's not very colorful, I'm afraid. Maybe you could make up a word for it.

Whatever you do, don't make us crackheads. That's just disgusting.

31

It's like you think you can do anything. And you remember that feeling afterwards, not how burnt you were; that's what makes you want to do it again. It's psychological that way.

I never learned to hit myself. Lamont did all of that. At first it was just on weekends. Saturday after lunch, he'd say, "Where you want to go?"

"Anywhere," I'd say.

And he'd say, "How fast you want to get there?"

It's like sex, your body anticipates it. Lamont would get everything together to cook it up. He just flicked his lighter and I was wet. I sat on the edge of our bed, watching the spoon go black and the bubbles popping. It was like he did it slow on purpose to get me going. He drew it into the syringe, and I could feel my blood moving, trying to get into position.

I didn't even want to see it. I laid my arm on the night table and looked at the wallpaper, the seam where the pattern nearly matched. He tapped the inside of my elbow and plumped up a vein.

"You okay?" he checked. It was a ritual, the last chance to bail.

"Dandy," I said, and he drove the spike home.

You want me to describe that first rush. It's like a flood. It's like standing on the front of a train flying down a mountainside. It's like you've been sick for the longest time and suddenly you're all better. You feel really lucky. It's almost funny how lucky you feel. It makes you laugh.

Your skin tingles all over, like a light sunburn. We'd spend the first hour in bed, Lamont going over me slowly. I'd just lie there with my eyes closed and tell him what he was doing to me. He liked that, when you talked. He wanted to know how he was doing. It was nice; even on Saturday, Casa Mia was empty in the middle of the afternoon. Only once did the neighbors complain, and that's because I was hitting the wall with the back of my head. Lamont liked to talk too. He used a lot of unnecessary language, which I thought was very sexy at the time. Natalie was the same way.

We'd take a shower together and get dressed and go out driving and look at things, wash the car, maybe pick up some cigarettes on the way back. You'd go through two or three packs and not even know it. You'd light one and find a new one burning in the ashtray. Nothing did anything to you, it's like you were superhuman. You'd drink a six of Miller and all it would do was make you go. And forget food, you didn't even want to think about it.

You could concentrate, but only on little things, and only for a short time. I used to write down what I wanted to get done while I was up. Because you have all this energy. The problem is you get distracted. You'll be doing the dishes and the next thing you know you've got all the spices down from the cupboard and you're putting them in order. You start cleaning the closet and end up with three flashlights in pieces on the kitchen table.

Five or six hours later you want to crash but you can't. It's like *Insomnia*, it just drags on. Your mouth tastes like an ashtray and you haven't eaten since breakfast and you know you've still got another two hours to go.

Physically it's hard on you, that's why you can't do it on a regular basis. You can't live on it. Back then I weighed about half of what I do now. The first time my mom brought Gainey in to see me, she didn't recognize me. My face was just bones. It wears you down. You chew your fingernails, you grind your teeth. You scratch your arms raw and then pick at the scabs. It's just not a very attractive drug.

But those first few hours, it's like you're there. You're fifty feet tall and your nerves are made out of gold. It's like you and the world are going exactly the same speed. When the sun's hot on the dashboard and there's no one on the road and you've got the whole day in front of you, it's like you're going to live forever.

32

That was exactly what it says it was for—obstructing justice. May was just when I was sentenced; I was actually arrested in December.

It was before Christmas. I'd gone to this Christmas party for everyone who worked at the Village Inn and this guy A.J. drove me home. I was late and forgot to call Lamont and when I got home he wasn't happy, half because I'd been drinking.

A.J. stayed outside in his car to make sure I got in okay, and Lamont didn't like the way I waved to him. I explained that he was a friend from work, but Lamont wouldn't let it drop. All I wanted to do was get in bed.

"He's just a good friend," I said.

"Now he's a *good* friend," he said. "How come I never heard of this good friend until tonight?" He said some other things he didn't mean, and I was too drunk to let them slide. It was silly, really.

"Look," I said, "can we talk about this tomorrow?"

"We're talking about this now," he said. When I walked past him into the bedroom, he pointed at my face and told me not to walk away.

I locked the door on him.

He was slapping it and yelling all kinds of stuff and I was yelling back sometimes—really unnecessary stuff, telling each other what kind of people we were, what was wrong with each other. We didn't really mean it. Finally he started kicking the door in. It was so cheap his foot came right through it, which of course he blamed on me. I just sat on the bed and laughed.

Someone downstairs called the cops. By the time they

knocked on the door we were done fighting; we just weren't talking to each other.

The woman cop took me into the bedroom.

"We were just having a discussion," I said.

"Looks like a good one," she said, pointing her pen at the door.

"He didn't touch me," I said.

"You've had a little to drink tonight, is that right?"

"Not much," I said. "Two beers."

I gave her all the information. No, he'd never struck me before. No, he had no prior history of drug usage.

When we came out to the living room, Lamont had cuffs on.

"Thanks a lot, Marjorie," he said.

"He never touched me," I kept telling them, but the guy was steering him toward the door. I got in his way.

"I can't believe you'd do this to me," Lamont said. I was crying, my nose was running all over the place.

"Ma'am, step aside," the woman said. "Ma'am, I'm only going to tell you this once. I don't think you want to go to jail tonight."

I just wanted to kiss him, to tell him everything was all right between us.

"I'll come down and get you out," I said. "Okay?"

"That's it," the woman said, "you're gone."

She grabbed me by the shoulder, spun me around and pushed my face into the wall. Lamont was shouting now. The woman bent one arm up behind my back and snapped the cuff on. Before she could get my other wrist, Lamont bowled her over and all four of us were on the floor.

"Marjorie," Lamont called.

"I'm okay," I said, because I was then.

If you have the mug shot, you can see where she pushed me into the wall. Look how full my face is. We'd only just started snorting it. Look how young we look. That was December of '84. I was twenty then. It seems a lot longer.

That was one reason my mom wasn't talking to me when I was living with Rico. When we were drinking, we used to beat on each other. We used to throw things. The toaster, the remote—it was just crazy. One time when I was in the emergency room, they called my mom to come pick me up. Rico and me had been fighting over him seeing this other girl from his work, and I told my mom that was it, I was leaving him.

I was just mad, and when I calmed down I tried to explain to her why I was going back. She didn't even try to understand. She only saw that *he* hit *me*. We had this huge fight, and she begged me not to go back to him. She said I was being stupid and that he'd kill me and all this other stuff, and finally she said that as long as I was with him she wasn't going to speak to me.

"Fine," I said, "I don't need this kind of stuff anyway."

And in the end she was wrong, that wasn't why we broke up at all. We broke up because Rico got in a bad accident one night in his old Grand Prix and didn't get hurt. It was raining and he was coming home from the Golden Corral. He was coming up Classen when this guy in an Imperial pulled out into his lane. Rico swerved to miss him and lost it and hit a telephone pole going sideways.

The Grand Prix was totaled. The steering column snapped off the headrest. Rico told me he woke up in the passenger seat. He didn't have his belt on or anything. There wasn't a cut on him, nothing. And right then and there he started to believe in Jesus.

Is that funny? He started to believe Jesus was looking out for him that night and he started to read the Bible. Before he came to bed he'd get down on his knees and pray. Sunday he'd get dressed up and go to church alone, and I'd just watch him. We fought about it. I thought he'd gone crazy. That's what it's like, it completely changes you and nobody who hasn't been through it understands. I didn't. One Sunday when he was in church, I packed up my things and left. That's when I moved in with Joy and Garlyn. I didn't tell my mom I'd left. I was still waiting for her to call me.

33

I didn't do anything while I was pregnant with Gainey, no booze, no drugs, not even cigarettes. Maybe a drag here and there, that was it. All of a sudden I couldn't stand the taste of them.

All I did was eat. I drank whole gallons of milk. My belly button popped when I was just six months. We'd go to Beverly's Pancake Kitchen for Sunday brunch; walking in it was like Jack Sprat and his wife. Lamont would order the short stack while I'd have the chicken-in-the-rough and a Black Cow followed by a slice of 7-Up pie, and he wouldn't say a word.

I was worried that my drinking might do something to the baby, that my body was already too messed up from the speed. The first time I went to the doctor I was afraid she'd see the tracks on my arms. The pamphlets she gave me didn't help. I kept seeing pictures of babies with just skin where their eyes were supposed to go. I remembered those calves in the sideshow tent with six or seven legs. I'd have these dreams where the doctor pulled something that looked like a starfish out of me. I'd wake up screaming and Lamont would hold me.

He was so sweet, putting up with me. We had a water bed, and I couldn't get out of it by myself, so he'd help me. I couldn't get up from the couch without him giving me a hand. Anything I wanted, he'd get for me.

"You want something?" he'd say. "What do you need?"

When I first found out, I was worried. I wasn't sure Lamont wanted kids. We'd never really talked about it, and I didn't know, with him being a foster kid. I didn't tell him the day I did the test. The plus turned pink and I threw the little plastic case into the sink so hard that it cracked. I waited until Friday, when we both got paid, and I made him a nice steak and a baked potato. I put a tablecloth on and made sure I looked good.

When I called him in from the TV, he stopped and looked at the table.

"What's the occasion?" he said.

"Nothing," I said, but he was looking at me like something was wrong, and I couldn't help it, I started to cry. I pushed past him into the bedroom and slammed the door.

"Marjorie!" he called. "What's wrong?"

"What do you think is wrong?" I said. "I'm pregnant."

I could hear his work boots on the floor in the hall but he didn't say anything. I lay there across the bed, waiting.

"Well?" I shouted. "Are we going to kill it?"

"That's up to you," he said.

"It's not up to me. It's yours too."

"Do you want to have it?" he said.

"What do *you* want to do?"

"Let me in," he said, and I got up and unlocked the door.

He laid down and put his arms around me and I knew we'd be okay.

Every night he rubbed my back, and when I couldn't get to sleep he'd stay up and talk with me. Sometimes I'd cry. My hormones were going all over.

"Are you happy?" I'd ask. "Are you sure?"

"I'm sure," he said.

And I was terrible to him. When I was crying and he asked me if I was all right, I screamed at him. I said he cared more about his car than he did about me. I took all the books I could find out of the library and made him look at the pictures. It was easy for him, I said; it only took guys five minutes to have a baby.

I was scared because I didn't know what it was going to be like. My mom was talking to me again because of it; she tried to tell me I'd know what to do when the time came. I didn't believe her.

"I know it hurts," I said, "but what does it hurt like?"

"I don't know," my mom said. "It's not the kind of pain you remember."

"Is it like a sharp pain that goes away or a dull pain that just stays there and grows?"

"Stop working yourself up," she said. "It's a natural process. Your body will know what to do. Just be thankful you've got my hips."

I know it was supposed to help, but all I could picture was my pelvis snapping like a wishbone.

Everything she said scared me. First I'd feel my water break and run hot down my legs. Between then and the delivery I had to worry about infection. Sometimes the baby could get sideways or strangle on its own cord. Sometimes when the head didn't crown right they had to cut you. And then there was the whole C-section thing. In the diagram they made it look like opening one of those little cereals you eat right in the box.

"Don't worry," my mom said. "There's nothing you can do about it anyway."

That was the problem, I wanted to say; I felt helpless. I was getting bigger and bigger and the time was going by so slowly. We'd picked names and I'd had a shower and we'd bought a crib. We did the amnio and it was okay; it was a boy, so we started calling my belly Gainey. It was summer and uncomfortable. Now just standing hurt. It got to the point where Lamont and me had to stop making love. I flipped the calendar and there was my due date circled in red. It was like now, I was just waiting for this thing to happen to me. It was coming and there was nothing I could do.

And for everyone else it wasn't a big deal. My doctor, my mom—they'd all been through it before, they knew everything that was going to happen, but that didn't tell *me* how it was going to feel.

I'd cry and Lamont would tell me everything was going to be all right, but I could tell he was scared too. I said he didn't have to be in the delivery room and then in the middle of the night one night I changed my mind and made him promise.

My doctor got my due date wrong by two weeks. It was supposed to be July 4th, which we thought was neat, but it turned out to be the 19th. We were ready to go that whole time, we had a bag packed and everything. When I finally went into labor we were relieved.

It was right after dinner on the 18th. We had take-out from Johnny's Char-broiler. I was on the couch watching something and my stomach just started to cramp. It was like I had to go so bad but I couldn't. Your muscle hurts like a charley horse; the best thing is not to fight it but that's your instinct. It hits you and then goes away, but you know it's coming around again. Lamont called my doctor. My water hadn't broken so she said not to come in until my contractions were seven to ten minutes apart. Lamont took his watch off to time them.

We watched TV until midnight, and they were still twenty minutes apart.

"You should get some rest," I told Lamont, but he said he was okay. He was drinking my diet Pepsis and smoking up a storm. I could barely stand the smell.

The late movie was *Alien.* Lamont clicked it over to Letterman.

We were sitting there about ten minutes later when the backs of my thighs felt wet. I looked down and the couch was soaked. I kept apologizing while Lamont called.

He'd backed the Roadrunner into its spot so we could take

off. He put two towels down on my seat and helped me in. He started the engine and flicked on the lights, released the emergency brake and rolled out of the lot. It was like a robbery; we hardly said anything. I'd never seen him take Choctaw so slowly. There was nobody out, but he was careful to signal, and careful of his mirrors.

The doctor wasn't there yet, and the nurse made us wait in a room with another woman who was crying between contractions. They hooked me up to a machine to measure mine. The lines looked like earthquakes. I tried to relax, but every time one hit I'd clench my stomach like I could stop it.

"You're doing great," Lamont said.

"How many minutes was that?" I said.

"Fifteen?"

"No," I said. "That's wrong."

The other woman was crying.

"Be quiet!" I said.

Finally the doctor showed up. When she pushed her hands into my belly, she yawned coffee breath right in my face.

"I can give you something for the pain," she said.

"I don't want any drugs," I said, partly afraid she'd see my tracks.

Two hours later, I was pleading with her for a shot.

"I thought you wanted it to be natural," Lamont reminded me.

"Didn't you hear what I just said?" I screamed. "Now give me the shot."

He came back in this stupid blue mask and I laughed at him. A contraction caught me by surprise and I started to cry. The doctor checked to see how dilated I was; her fingers searched and it hurt. The orderlies came and moved me onto a gurney and clapped the rails up.

The doctor was wearing blue too, and there was a tent of it

around my legs. There was a mirror I could look in but I didn't. I still didn't know what to do, and I said so.

"You're okay," the doctor said. "I just need you to keep pressing down. Dad, can you get that arm? Okay, here we go."

I was too tired to push, and then I held my breath and tried. The lights made me sweat but I was still cold.

"A little more," she said, like I wasn't trying.

"Come on," she said. "You can do it, Mom."

I gritted my teeth and said some unnecessary things.

"There," she said. "Great. Okay. You're all done. You can relax now."

"You did it," Lamont was saying. He had my hand.

"I think you're going to be very happy," the doctor said.

It was okay, I thought, I could die now. There was nothing left of me.

The nurse brought Gainey to me in a blue blanket and put him on my chest.

He was moving his little hands. His eyes were closed but his mouth was open like a baby bird's. He had hair, he even had tiny eyebrows.

"Well, look at you," I said. "So you're the one who's been causing all this trouble."

34

Sorry, I'm getting a little ahead of myself there. I start telling that story and I can't stop.

We were married before I started to show. It's not hard to figure out, all you have to do is count backwards. I won't lie; a lot of things overlap in here, like me already being pregnant at that Christmas party, or the other arrest. I'm sure you've got that too.

What's important is that we stuck together through all of that stuff.

Sister Perpetua says love endures, and that's what Lamont and me did—we endured each other. I still am. After everything that happened, if he pulled up and opened that door for me again, I'd still get in.

It's funny though. When I'm driving, I'm always by myself.

I never thought I'd get married. I never thought I'd have a kid. These weren't things I wanted right then. They weren't things I'd think about the way some girls I knew did. It was all kind of a surprise.

Lamont proposed to me at the Saturday flea market at the Sky-Vue Drive-In. We were at this booth where this old guy sold knives and cast-iron skillets and bleached steer skulls. Him and his wife sat in plastic lawn chairs under a canopy off of their camper; they never got up unless you had your money out. They had a bunch of old campaign buttons and pocket watches and Mexican coins in a glass-topped box, and in there was this pearl ring. The pearl had colors all swirled around in it, the way oil makes a rainbow on water.

"That's pretty," I said, to see what Lamont thought.

"How much is it?" he said.

The little tag was turned over.

Lamont got the man up. His hands were big, his fingers square as fish sticks.

"Four hundred dollars," he said, and held the glass top open like it was a question.

"Can we see it?" Lamont said. I don't know why; we couldn't afford it.

The man pinched it up by the band.

Lamont tried to take it with two fingers but he missed. It dropped in the dust under the table, and he knelt down to look for it. He had it before I could help him, but he didn't get up. He stayed there on one knee and held the ring out to me. And then he proposed. He said it just like you always hear.

People walking by were staring at us. People stopped. The old man's wife got up from her chair to see better. I didn't know what to say. We'd been fighting all week about how I hadn't told my mom yet, and now here he was being sweet. It was his baby, he knew that. I did love him. He was all I had.

"Yes," I said, "I will," and the people around us clapped.

Lamont slipped the ring on my finger, price tag and all. I still have that tag. It's going to go to Gainey. I'm keeping the ring.

When I told my mom, she didn't say anything at first. I had to repeat it.

"I heard you," she said. "I'm just trying to think."

"We're going to have a baby."

"I knew there was a reason," she said. "I was hoping that wasn't it. What does this boy do?"

It was going okay, I thought. She could have just hung up.

"Will you come?" I asked her.

"It would be nice if I had a little warning."

We didn't say anything then.

"Of course I will," she said. "What kind of mother would miss her daughter's first wedding?"

"So?" Lamont said when I got off.

"She's coming."

"Is that what you want?"

"Of course," I said. "Why wouldn't I?"

That Friday we got married at Edmond City Hall. My mom gave me her dress. It was yellowed and smelled of mothballs but it fit. Lamont rented a tux. We picked up my mom on the way. She wore blue, and hadn't had her hair tinted. I flipped the seat up so she could get in back. She reached between us to shake Lamont's hand.

"Nice to meet you," he said.

"Just don't be like the last one," she said.

Lamont gave me a look, and I shrugged like I didn't know what was going on. I knew we'd fight about it that night, but right then I didn't want to get into it. Nothing was going to ruin my wedding day.

We were there early. My mom was our only witness so we borrowed the lady from the Traffic Bureau. In the pictures she's the only one smiling.

35

We decided on Las Vegas for our honeymoon, but we didn't have enough money. We got all the maps and tour books from the Triple A, and at night after work we'd lay them out on the coffee table and go.

"The Sahara," I'd say.

And Lamont would go, "We're playing seven-card stud and drinking Jack and Coca-Cola."

"Pepsi."

"Okay. We're at the Sands—"

"We're playing blackjack and eating the free sandwiches. We're at the Flamingo—"

"We're winning. We've got all these silver dollars from hitting the slots, and instead of blowing it, we go upstairs and pour them all over the bed."

"Then what?" I'd say, and he'd pick me up and carry me into the bedroom and kick the door shut behind us.

After a while, we didn't even make it to Vegas. We'd get off 40 and stop at the Petrified Forest or the Painted Desert or the Grand Canyon. The overlooks were empty, the sunset throwing shadows. We stopped in the middle of Hoover Dam and climbed onto the roof and pulled off each other's shorts. Lamont's bikinis fell until we couldn't see them. The vinyl was warm against my back. Lake Mead was upside down and blue.

"I love you, Marjorie," he said. "I love you so much."

And I believed him. Because it was true then.

36

I wouldn't say my relationship with my mom got better while I was pregnant. We talked now, and sometimes I'd visit her, but she wouldn't come to our apartment and she wouldn't talk to Lamont. Whenever he answered the phone, she'd ask if I was there, and if I wasn't, she wouldn't stay on. She called him "he" and "that boy of yours," as in "What would your father think of that boy of yours?"

She came to Casa Mia just once, for my shower. Garlyn was drunk and spilled the guacamole on the carpet. She started bawling and swabbing at it with her hands.

"I'm sorry," she said, "I'm just losing one of my best friends in the whole world."

My mom swooped in with a wooden spoon and a bowl. In the kitchenette, she said, "I can't believe anyone would come to something this nice in that condition."

"She's my friend," I said. "And that *is* her condition."

"She reminds me of someone we both knew before she cleaned up her act."

"My life is not an act," I said.

"That's not what I meant, and you know it."

We both said some things then. The kitchenette was right next to the living room, there was a bar in between. Garlyn came over to apologize; she was still crying. She wanted to hug my mom but I got in between them.

"I don't know what you're thinking," my mom said later. She

was on her knees, scrubbing at the green stain. "You're not doing her any favors by putting up with it."

"What am I supposed to do, write her off?"

"Are you saying that's what I did with you?"

"I'm not saying anything," I said. "Why is it that every time we talk about anything it always comes back to me and you?"

She quit and walked past me and ran water onto the sponge. "I don't know why you invited me here if you're just going to treat me this way."

"What way?"

"Maybe it would be better if we just spoke to each other on the phone."

"Maybe it would," I said.

She got her purse and checked to make sure she had exact change for the bus. "Well," she said at the door, "it's been pleasant."

"For both of us," I said.

But here, listen to this. Out of everyone, my mom was the only one who came to my trial. Every day she had a new outfit on and her hair looked just done. Mr. Jefferies said it was important to show the jury that I had people who believed in me, and he called her and she came. She got a babysitter for Gainey and sat right behind us in the first row with the people Mr. Jefferies hired. And she didn't have to, she could have just stayed home.

I'd see her on TV, trying to get through all the cameramen, trying to smile. Mr. Jefferies said she didn't have to answer their questions but she did. She said some of the nicest things about me on TV.

I remember once she said, "Even if she did all those things they say she did, she is still my daughter."

And I think she meant it, no matter what happened after that.

I think she'll be awake at midnight, listening to KOMA's live broadcast from outside the main gate. She'll be waiting for Mr. Jefferies to call.

And then what will she do? Will she turn the light off and roll over and look at the moon? Will she sit there with the light on and open the Bible I sent her? She could do anything. She could go downstairs and make a sandwich at the kitchen table. She could walk out into the backyard and fall on her knees in the grass. But she won't. I know my mom enough to expect something quiet and private that makes sense to her. Something dignified.

There's a phone here I'm allowed to use, and when it gets close I'll call her. Three years ago when I was close, she answered and said she had nothing to say to me. I scared her, I think, after all those years. I don't expect anything different now, but it would be cruel not to.

I know what I'll say—the same thing as last time. "It wasn't your fault," I'll say. "You did everything you could. Mom," I'll say, "I love you." And I won't wait then. I won't hurt both of us. I'll just say goodbye and hang up.

37

See, I knew you'd have this one too. Mr. Jefferies tried to use this at the trial. I didn't want him to, but he said it was our best chance. Even though we were both arrested that time, he said the jury would blame Lamont because he was a man. It was even better that I was pregnant then. He was afraid my pictures wouldn't be admitted as evidence. He didn't expect the prosecution to use Lamont's.

The report doesn't say what started it, it just says "domestic disturbance." That was a big question during the trial, but since Mr. Jefferies didn't want me on the stand, no one could answer it. What started the disturbance is that Lamont found a pint of Popov's in my bag. I knew it was wrong but I was so low, just sitting in the apartment all day, waddling downstairs to the hot laundry room. I needed something to keep me going.

I was in the kitchen making dinner when he came up behind me.

"What's this?" he said, and held up the bottle.

I looked at it and all I saw was the two inches I wasn't going to get to drink.

"Must be an old one," I said.

"It was in your purse."

"What were you doing in my purse?"

"Don't lie to me," he said. He leaned in to smell my breath, and I pushed him away. I had a big slotted spoon in my hand for the string beans, and when he grabbed my other arm, I hit him with it.

He ripped it out of my hand and slapped me, knocking me back against the stove. I got ahold of the kettle and bonked him on the shoulder; the water went all over the place. I threw the kettle at his face and ran for the bedroom.

"I don't know where you think you're going," he called after me, because the door was gone; the landlord never fixed it.

I grabbed the lamp from the nightstand and threw it just as he came in. He was ready for me; he had a folding chair like a lion tamer. The lamp shattered against it. He dropped it and covered his face, swearing. There was blood between his fingers.

I groped in the drawer and came up with a flashlight.

"Why do you want to fight?" I said. I was crying and holding the flashlight up like a club.

He was still holding his face. I didn't think he could see, so I tried to run by him.

He caught hold of my blouse. I twisted and it ripped, and I had to hit him. The third time, the top of the flashlight came off and the batteries flew out. One of them cracked the mirror on the headboard. Lamont fell half onto the bed and rolled off, one arm caught underneath him. There was blood in his hair but I didn't stick around to see if he was all right.

I ran downstairs to our landlord Mrs. Wertz and banged on her door, but she wouldn't answer. Finally some old guy down the hall stuck his head out and said she was with the police over in B building. They were there because someone was fighting.

They were in the parking lot behind B. They had a guy in the back of the car and the gal with them, holding a towel to her mouth. When the first cop saw me, he said, "You with her?"

They made me stand on the landing while they went in to get Lamont. They had their guns out and everything. A minute later, one of them came back.

"Is he all right?" I said.

"I'm going to have to ask you to turn around," he said.

"Is he okay?"

"He's unconscious, ma'am. Now if you'll place your hands behind your head with your fingers knitted together."

They arrested Lamont too, but he got to go to Baptist. That's why his picture is him on the stretcher. I was arraigned and made bail in time to be there when he woke up.

He had a bandage around his head like a soldier. They said one cheekbone was broken and he had a concussion but otherwise he was fine. The skin around his eyes was the color of grape jelly, and sitting there looking at him, I swore that I would hurt the person that had done this to him, that somehow I would get rid of her.

38

How did our life change after the baby? We were busier. We didn't sleep or make love as much, and I was stuck at home while Lamont got to go to work. It was quiet, and I got to read a lot, but the only people I talked to all day were clients who came by for an eighth and stayed five minutes.

Gainey wouldn't take my milk, and that was a hard thing. I was tired of being thrown up on. My stomach was mush; my breasts hurt. In a weird way, I wished I was still pregnant. I started smoking again, and I knew Lamont was going through my shoeboxes. He was good about changing Gainey and feeding him dinner, but the baths and the laundry and all the rest of it was up to me. When Gainey cried in the middle of the night, Lamont wasn't good enough for him. My mom said I was lucky, that my dad never touched a diaper.

"I'm sorry," Lamont said, "I wish I didn't have to go to work either."

"It's when you *are* here," I said. "That's when I need your help."

He'd remember for a little bit, then he'd go back to ignoring me.

One day he came home while Gainey was taking a nap and found me crying on the couch. I couldn't stop.

"What happened?" he asked. "Marjorie, what's wrong?"

He held me by the shoulders and looked at me like I'd gone crazy, and I felt sorry for him, stuck with a crazy woman.

"What's wrong?" he said.

It was just my life, I wanted to say, but then he'd say he loved me and that we had a beautiful baby—things I couldn't feel bad about. How could I explain that that was why I was crying?

"Marjorie," he said, "come on."

"I don't know," I finally said. "I don't know. Nothing. I'm just tired."

It got better when Gainey started sleeping through the night, but still I felt tired all the time. When he went down for his afternoon nap, I'd take a carton of ice cream down from the freezer and skim a line off the top of an eighth and lay it out on the coffee table. You'd feel it pinch in the back of your nose and then drip down your throat all bitter. I'd put the stereo on low and run in place for half an hour, then do two hundred sit-ups. Before my shower I'd weigh myself and check my stomach in the mirror. The water there was great in the middle of the day. I'd turn it up as hot as I could stand.

Right there's two things I miss — privacy and water pressure.

Gainey would be getting up just as I finished drying my hair. I'd see if he needed changed, and then we'd play on the couch until Lamont got home.

"Anything happen here?" Lamont would ask, and I'd tell him who came by. At dinner I'd push my food around till you could see the middle of the plate. I did the dishes, so he never caught on.

I started doing two lines, then three. Instead of skimming, I just kept an eighth for myself and raised the price. It took him a few weeks to notice how flat my stomach was, and that was in bed; the next day he didn't say anything.

My mom did, though. I hadn't seen her in a month or so when I took Gainey over to Kickingbird Circle. It was April and in the eighties, so I wore shorts. The Underwoods already had their sprinklers going. I rang the bell. When she opened the door, she looked at Gainey first, then turned to me and just stopped.

"Oh my God," she said.

"What?" I said, cause she was staring. She touched my cheek like she couldn't see me.

"You're not drinking again."

"No," I said. "I'm all done with that."

"Then what is it—drugs?"

I laughed like she was being silly, and kissed her. I lied right to her face, though we both knew the truth.

39

The receiving stolen goods thing wasn't our fault. The stereo was actually ours; we bought it off these college kids in a van. The guy who gave us the wheels said he had a receipt for them. The same for the crossbow and the portable generator and the chain saws— we just thought he was cleaning out his garage.

They searched the entire place with a German shepherd. One guy even opened the ice cream before putting it back. We just sat there entertaining Gainey with the car keys. We both knew enough not to say anything. They took us down and booked us and finally they let us go. When we got home we discovered Lamont's best Meat Puppets bootleg had been in the tape player.

Our lawyer Ms. Tolliver said all they could give us was probation, and that's what we got. It was Lamont's fault, being nice. From then on we only dealt in cash.

40

I wouldn't call what happened a bust, it was more like an accident.

It was all my mom's fault. We'd gone to the mall to look at summer clothes for Gainey and we were coming home on Santa

Fe. She was driving her Riviera. Gainey was in the back in his car seat. I was always careful about that. He'd just thrown up, so I took my belt off and turned around to clean him up.

"Don't get in an accident," I said.

"I won't," my mom said.

Five seconds later I'm flying backwards into the dashboard. A piece of the windshield is stuck in my hair, and there's this yellow Granada two inches away from my face.

Gainey's screaming in the backseat, and my mom's glasses are snapped in half.

"I told you not to do that!" I said.

The driver of the Granada was an old man wearing a hat and a brown suit like it was the fifties. The ignition was buzzing cause his door had flown open. He didn't get out, he just sat there staring at the steam coming up from the antifreeze. It looked like he might be knocked out. Someone looked in my mom's window and asked if we were all right.

"No," I said, "we had an accident."

My back hurt, but I needed to see Gainey. I tried to pull myself up but my right hand wouldn't do what I wanted it to.

"I think my wrist is broken," I said.

"Don't move," my mom said. "You're not supposed to move."

My left hand was okay. Gainey's face was red but he seemed fine. I leaned over the seat and brushed the spit-up and glass off his tray. I tried to unbuckle him but I needed both hands.

"It's okay," I said.

My mom was crying. "Your father bought me this car."

"Will you please help me?" I said.

"Don't yell at me. I know you hate me but you don't have to yell at me." On her forehead was a red imprint of the steering wheel. A siren was coming.

I blame this on my mom, but right here I could of done something if I'd of been thinking, but I wasn't. I didn't know that my purse wasn't next to me on the seat where I'd left it. I had no idea that right then the eighth I'd been dreaming about all morning was lying on the street right outside my door.

A cop car pulled up and killed its siren. Gainey was done crying; he was just hiccupping. There were people all over the street, even one guy with a fire extinguisher. Traffic was jumping the curb to get around us.

There was only one cop in the car. He came up to my mom's window. His head was shaved like someone going out for football and he had a microphone Velcroed to his shoulder.

"Everyone okay here?" he said.

"He hit us," my mom said. "My light was green."

I told him about my wrist.

"All right," he said, and went around to check on the old man. "Sir," he said, "sir."

The old man was staring straight ahead like he didn't hear him.

"Sir!" the cop said, and waved a hand in front of his face. He didn't blink.

The cop knelt down and laid two fingers on the old man's throat, then walked back to his car and got a blanket from the trunk. We sat there listening to Gainey hiccup while the cop spread it over the old guy.

"It was green!" my mom said. "I saw it."

"I know," I said, though I could tell she wasn't sure anymore.

More sirens were coming—more cops, a fire truck, two ambulances. They parked right behind us in the middle of the street.

The cop got Gainey out, and this woman paramedic finally convinced my mom she could move. She stood up and all this glass fell out of her lap; the little cubes bounced on the ground like hail. I had to scoot across the seat to get out her door. Another cop I recognized from somewhere took me to an ambulance, where they looked at my wrist. My mom stood there with Gainey; they were both fine.

"Does this hurt?" the paramedic said, and twisted my hand.

"Yes!" I begged her.

There were forms to fill out. I couldn't write, so my mom had to do it. I lied about what medications I was taking. Just when we were getting ready to leave, the first cop came over with my purse and asked me if it was mine. I didn't think, I just took it and thanked him.

"How about this?" he said, and held up the eighth by one corner. "Do you recognize this?"

All I had to do was say no.

"Not again," my mom said. "Marjorie, why do you keep doing this?"

"So you do recognize it?"

"It's her husband—"

"Shut up," I said. "Just shut up, Mother. You've already killed one person today, isn't that enough?"

She started telling me how I was the one hurting everyone, and I started giving it back.

"Hold up, hold up," the cop shouted, and gave me a lecture on being a mother and why my mom was worried about me. My mom just stood there nodding, agreeing with him. Then he got out his little test kit. He was surprised when it turned orange. He thought it was cocaine, the dummy. He was looking for blue.

He read me my rights. I didn't say a word after that, I just looked at my mom like how could she do this.

"I'm not sorry," she said. "If you want me to say I'm sorry, I'm not going to."

"It's fine for you," she said, hefting Gainey, "but you've got to think about him."

The cop put us in his car to go to the hospital, me behind the cage, my mom and Gainey up front. My mom and the cop talked about heart attacks and how the old man could of been driving around dead like that for a while. We were all very lucky.

The emergency room took us first because I was under arrest. My mom had to fill out more forms. The cop left us alone for a minute while we waited for the doctor. I took Gainey from my mom with my good arm and sat there holding him close.

"You're the one doing this," my mom said, "not me."

The cop came back with the doctor, who looked at my arm. He actually bent down and looked at it like his eyes were bad. He had liver spots on his forehead and I could smell his hair cream.

"Tell me if this hurts," he said, but I grabbed my arm back. He jumped like I had a knife, and the cop got up.

"Trust me," I said. "It's broken."

"Do you want me to help you or not," the doctor said.

When he twisted it, I screamed in his ear.

It took a while, laying all the hot strips of gauze across it. It still hurt just as much.

Outside, the cop made sure my mom had money for a cab. He locked me in the back of the car and took Gainey's seat out and set it on the curb for her. They talked for a minute. My mom was thanking him, touching him on the arm.

He came around the front and got in. The cast was still warm in my lap. I knew she was looking at me, maybe waving, but I wouldn't look.

"You're not going to say goodbye?" the cop said.

"Just drive," I said, and finally he did.

Ms. Tolliver said I'd see some time—not much. Her best guess was six months, and that's exactly what the judge gave me. I couldn't believe it. I'd been arrested before, and I'd done a lot of things, but this was over nothing. I was going to jail. I knew I was but I didn't really believe it. It hit me all at once when the judge read the sentence and the bailiff came and took me by the arm.

My mom and Lamont were there, sitting in different places. While the bailiff was taking me away I looked over my shoulder at them like they could save me. But they couldn't.

41

I did my six months at Clara Waters. It wasn't really a jail the way you think of one. It was an old motel off I-35 they'd turned into a pre-release center. Clara Waters Community Corrections Center, they called it. It used to be the Planet Motel. They'd left all the furniture, the big mirrors in the bathrooms and the paintings screwed to the walls. You could still see the yellow fluorescents under the gutters and the big Saturn out front with all the neon gone. There were no bars on the windows or barbed wire on top of the fences. You could walk out anytime you liked.

The idea was that you wouldn't take off because you didn't have that much time left. Some of the gals had been in places like Mabel Bassett or Eddie Warrior for six or seven years and now they were getting out, so they were real careful. But most of us were in for prostitution or petty larceny, being an accessory to something. We were young and knew this was just temporary. There were a lot of mothers.

I remember the first night I was there. There were four of us in this motel room; Natalie hadn't come yet. We had our own bathroom and an air conditioner we could set any way we liked. The door wasn't locked. We were on the second floor, and you stepped out onto the balcony and there was a guard. Before lights-out they didn't even say anything to you, you could stand there and smoke. Down the highway was Frontier City, this big amusement park, and you could see the lights of the Ferris wheel through the trees. It was a big double one, the kind that flips over. You could almost hear the music. It made you think of fried dough stands and kids sticky with cotton candy. That first night I stood there and watched that Ferris wheel going around and thought of Gainey and I swore that this would never happen to me again.

After the first month, we were allowed out on work release. Your counselor gave you a day pass, and you went out and tried to find a job. If you got one, you could go out every day—seven days a week if you could prove you were working. But only during the day; at night you had to be back. And you had to tell your boss you were doing work release, you couldn't just not mention it.

My first day out I applied to three jobs and made love to Lamont five times. I applied to crummy places, thinking I could get something quick. I wanted a job I wouldn't want when I got out, something I could just dump. I'd worked enough crummy jobs to recognize one. I tried the chains first—Grandy's and Shoney's and the Waffle House—knowing they had high turnover.

I went out looking for a week, spending the afternoons at Mia Casa like everything was normal. Lamont was getting better at diapering Gainey. I liked having both of them in bed, the whole family close like that so I could smell them, touch their skin. It was hard to leave.

I applied to Hometown Buffet and Luby's and Furr's Cafeteria. I applied to Church's Chicken and Cocina de Mino. Burger King had a sign on the door that said, *Come in for your Whoppertunity.* I kept waiting for my counselor Mrs. Langer to call me into her office and tell me that someone had called, but no one did.

The problem was it was June and all the high schools were letting out, Mrs. Langer said. She reminded me of my old guidance counselor Mrs. Drake; she had plants in her office and all kinds of advice. Possibly my cast was scaring away potential employers. I just had to be tenacious. I might try applying to more places. I would, I said. You just nod and say yes to someone like that even though what they say never works.

Friday Lamont drove me around all day and waited for me in the parking lot. We didn't even make love. Dropping me off, he said something would turn up, and we got in a big argument. Weekends were the worst because I didn't get to see him, and I'd had enough. We both said some unnecessary things, and we didn't make it up. I just walked away from the car. Gainey was screaming in the backseat, and I thought, fine, let him deal with him.

Monday, Mrs. Langer gave me a card that said Coit's Root Beer Drive-In called. It was funny cause I even liked them. They were right across Northwest Expressway from Charcoal Oven. It was a real old-time drive-in with a fiberglass canopy and a speaker box on a pole at every stall. The main building was shaped like a keg and had things like TOASTED SANDWICHES and MALTS and SOFT DRINKS written around it in red and green neon. The carhops dressed like majorettes, in satin tops and two-toned skirts and white vinyl knee boots. The shakes came with whipped cream and a cherry. They even served Pepsi. It made me feel bad for yelling at Lamont.

My schedule worked out good. I had to be there at ten, so I'd get forty-five minutes with Lamont before work. He'd come in after lunch and park in one of the far stalls, and I'd take my break with him. The windows were so dark no one could see in. We'd put Gainey in the front seat and hop in back.

It was a fun job. I kind of missed working, all the talk. They called an order of fries a bag of rags. A yellow steak was a burger with mustard. "Walk a dog sideways," they'd say. "Float me a skinny Joe." The coffeemaker was a Bunn-O-Matic, so they called coffee Bunn mud. "Bunn me," they'd say, "Bunn me two."

Inside, you could hear the people in their cars. Once they buzzed for an order, the line stayed open. You'd hear them singing with the radio or fighting. That was the funniest, the mothers who buzzed. They'd be screaming at their kids, calling them all kinds of names, and you'd come on and all of a sudden their voices would get all nice. It was even better after I got Natalie a job there.

Sorry I'm going all over the place. I guess Darcy's stuff must be kicking in. You wanted me to describe Clara Waters.

Compared to here, Clara Waters was easy, but that was my first time in and I was a little frightened. There were some gals in there I thought were hard, though I don't think that now. They seemed that way to me because my life was easy then. I wouldn't put any of them up against Lucinda or even Darcy. They were headed in the right direction, the ones who'd been here or in Eddie Warrior. They were going home. I think that's why the state put us in with them; it was hoping they might teach us something that would keep us from ever getting here.

I remember going into the room for the first time. It was dumb but I was afraid I'd be the only white gal. It turned out I was, except the other three weren't black, they were Chinese. Two of them were cousins from this gang down around Mustang; the other was a hooker with only a month to go. One of cousins' names was Emily, which I thought was weird. They both had jean jackets and listened to their Walkmans constantly. Their English wasn't very good, and all the hooker did was read magazines. None of them paid any attention to me. I got the cot closest to the door, and when the hooker left we all moved down one.

There was everyone in there—black gals, Indians, Mexican gals, a lot of trailer trash. We all pretty much kept to ourselves in little groups; you could see it in the cafeteria. There weren't a lot of fights like you might think. I think with guys it's different.

If you have to have a fight, there was this tall gal named Barbara Something everyone was afraid of. She had something wrong with her; her head was too big, like a puppet. She knocked out a guard with a can of Cherry Crush and got sent here. But mostly it was quiet. People liked to sleep.

The food wasn't bad there, I remember that. It's not bad here either. They make two things here that are great—southern fried chicken and chicken-fried steak. I guess you can't go too far wrong with those anywhere in Oklahoma.

I don't know what else you want. They tore the place down in '92. Before that it went coed for a while, with the gals in one wing and the guys in the other two. I wish I'd been there for that. Maybe me and Natalie wouldn't have gotten together then. But I can't complain. I'd much rather be there than here.

42

Right, this is where I first met Natalie Kramer. She was my roommate for the last two months along with Emily and the other cousin. She was in for passing bad checks. You could see why people would take them from her. She looked nice—long cinnamon hair, brown eyes, medium all over. Pretty but not beautiful. Her teeth were straight and she kept her shoulders back, even when she was sitting. An Audrey Hepburn neck, nice shoes. She looked like someone I might have grown up with on Kickingbird Circle, someone who'd gone to college and gotten married.

That first day she walked into the room, Emily and her cousin didn't bother to take off their headphones. Natalie took one step in and stopped like she might not be allowed. She had jeans and a T-shirt on, but they looked too neat, like she wasn't used to them. Her earrings were just gold studs; she didn't wear any rings and her nails were perfect. She made a point of shaking my hand. She waved to the cousins; they looked at each other like she was nuts.

"Is this one mine?" she asked, then sat down with her bag across her lap, hugging it like a dog. "I can't believe I'm here," she said, and started to cry. The cousins giggled.

"It's okay," I said, "I know how it is."

She had a mini pack of tissues with her and she wiped her eyes. "Is there a bathroom?"

I pointed to the door.

She locked it behind her. When she finally came out, the cousins had gone to supper. Natalie apologized and thanked me for being so kind. "I was afraid there wouldn't be anyone nice here," she said. "I'm afraid I'm just a big baby."

"It's okay," I said. "So am I."

I took her to supper and sat with her, but she couldn't eat. It was her boyfriend, an older guy; he'd left and cleared out their account. She'd just been laid off and her landlord wouldn't let her out of the lease. Looking back, it was probably all lies. It didn't matter. She was already my friend.

She went to take a bite of mashed potatoes, then put it down again. She just sat there looking at her tray. It was like the kind for a TV dinner except there was no square for your dessert.

"Come on," I said, "try some of the chicken." I even speared a piece for her.

That night when the cousins were asleep, Natalie thanked me. She reached across the gap between our cots and squeezed my hand.

"What are you in for?" she asked, and I told her some of it, not the whole thing. Her mother was just like that, she said, and told me about her boyfriend coming to Easter supper drunk and knocking the ham onto the carpet. We laughed and one of the cousins shifted and we quieted down. His name was Don and he was in auto parts. He was fine when he wasn't drinking, but this was the last time. It was too crazy, it was like a roller coaster. One time he shoved her head in the microwave and tried to turn it on. Another time he turned the hose on her while she was sleeping.

"You're married," she said, and pointed to my ring. "You don't have to deal with that garbage."

"Thank God," I said.

She was from Yukon. She'd come to the city to go to school and ended up dropping out after a few semesters.

"Same here," I said, and we talked about college. It turned out she'd worked at a Conoco. We traded drive-off stories. She remembered sprinkling the measuring stick with Comet before dipping it in the tanks so you could read the level better.

"This is so funny," she said.

It was two-thirty. "Better save some for tomorrow," I said.

"Marjorie," she said, and took my hand again. "Thank you."

"It's no big thing," I said. "The first day's always the hardest."

She took her hand back and we lay there quiet for a while. You could hear the trucks going by on 35, headed south to Dallas and San Antone, north to Wichita and Kansas City. Even then I liked to drive in my mind. North of the city there was nothing for three or four exits. At night all you could see were the big radio antennas, the lights blinking to keep the planes away.

"Hey," Natalie whispered. "What's the other one's name?"

"I don't know," I said. "I can't pronounce it."

"And why Emily?"

We started to talk again, and suddenly it was four o'clock. We had to get up in three hours. Still, we didn't stop, and as I drifted off to her voice I thought that this was what it must be like to have a sister.

That morning she unpacked her bathroom stuff in front of the mirror. She'd brought everything—conditioner, perfume, razors. She had a makeup case full of lipsticks, foundation, an eyelash curler. She had a purple velour jewelry roll full of gold chains. I closed the door so the cousins wouldn't see it all.

"I wouldn't flash that stuff around," I said.

"They said I could keep it."

"That's the kind of stuff that disappears around here."

"Oh," she said, and packed it up again.

"Why did you bring so much stuff anyway?"

"I didn't have anywhere to leave it," she said. "I don't think it's a lot."

"What about your mom and dad?"

She laughed, just a single "Ha!" It was the first time I'd seen her angry.

"If you want, I can keep it at my place. I can stick it in my purse when I leave for work."

"I don't know," she said.

"If that's all I had in the world, I definitely wouldn't leave it in this room."

"You're right," she said. And she didn't have to trust me then, but she did. She just handed me the whole thing.

At work, I unrolled the purple velour in the storeroom to see what there was. It wasn't much: a few chains, some freshwater pearls, a bunch of cheap earrings—nothing really worth stealing.

"What's all this?" Lamont said when I showed him. I had all of it on under my uniform. He broke one of the chains while we made love, and I felt bad. I'd get it fixed.

"What kind of idiot is she?" he asked when we were done.

"Don't talk like that," I said. "She's my friend."

Back at Clara Waters, Natalie was waiting for me. She'd

sneaked a piece of pecan pie out of the cafeteria for me. She wanted to know how everything went, if it was okay with Lamont. Her day had been bad. She'd tried to sleep but she could hear the drums from the cousins' Walkmans. We shared a cigarette out on the balcony. The Ferris wheel swung above the trees.

"I don't see how I'm going to do this for three months," she said.

"It's not so bad once you start your work release. I'll put in a good word for you if you want."

"I do," she said. "Thanks."

She gave me the butt back for the last hit.

"He thought you were crazy," I said, "trusting me."

"I'd rather trust you than anybody else here."

"Is that good?" I said.

"I don't know," she said. "It's something."

In prison, you make friends quick or not at all. When I wasn't at work, I was with her. Even the cousins were jealous of us. She saved me when I ran out of tampons. When my hairbrush died, she let me use hers. We both took a size 8, so we could borrow each other's tops. I gave her my rice pudding and she gave me her canned pears. I envied her legs; she wanted my waist. Nights we talked on the balcony until lights-out, then went inside and passed a butt, an ashtray on the floor between our cots. She had no man, no baby, no plans. I think I wanted her life, or my old life back. Maybe I just wanted to start over, go.

I helped fill out her application for Coit's. It was the only place we were going to apply. She could skate but she'd never been a waitress.

"What's your favorite restaurant?" I said.

"Interurban."

"That's good," I said like Mrs. Langer.

"You're not putting that down?"

"You want the job, right?"

"Yeah."

"They'll never check," I said.

At work I made sure her application was on top of Ned's clipboard. He called me into the storeroom to discuss it. It was short. Ned liked me too much to argue. I could make him do anything.

"And she skates," I said.

"Don't beg," Ned said. "I was going to hire her all along. We don't have to pay you gals minimum wage."

When I told Natalie, she hugged me. We were out on the balcony, and the guard turned away from us. I'd been borrowing Nat's shampoo, and she smelled like me. "Thank you," she said, "thank you so much," and her body started to shake against mine. "I don't know what I'd do without you."

"It's okay," I said, but she wouldn't stop.

The lights on the far wing went out, and then around the balcony toward us until we were standing in the dark.

"It's time," I said. "Come on, let's go to bed."

43

Describe Natalie.

A liar.

That pretty much says it. I could say worse but it wouldn't be Christian.

She was prettier than she looked at first, and smarter. She always kept a little in reserve. She was always acting, always trying to get something from you. She was like one of those kids in school who cause all the trouble and then act all innocent when the teacher shows up. But she was pretty and she could get away with it. You always felt sorry for her. She always had some sort of story.

<h1 style="text-align:center">44</h1>

It's true. I never said it was or wasn't because I don't think it's that important. It's personal anyway. And it didn't happen the way Natalie says in her book. There was no dope and no candle; I don't know where she got that from. And I wasn't the one who started it, that should be clear.

That would have been in August, because Natalie had been there for more than a month. We were both working at Coit's by then. She'd cover for me when I was late coming back from break with Lamont. She could really skate; people would ask special for her. Her skates laced up above the ankle and made her calves look like she was wearing heels. You could see the people in their cars watch her as she rolled past.

We came back on the van that night. You always felt gross from all the grease in the air there. The first thing you wanted to do was take a shower. We took turns going first, and tonight was my night. I got undressed and turned on the water and let it get hot. Natalie came in to use the john. We were talking about tomorrow, getting paid or something, just talk. The water was hot, so I pulled the knob for the shower and got in. We talked over the water.

"Don't flush," I said.

"I won't," she said.

She kept talking but I couldn't hear anything while I was doing my hair, and I said so. It was the best time of the day because the water was hot; if you tried it in the morning you got about a minute and then it was freezing. I leaned back to rinse and felt a cool breeze on my front. My eyes were closed, and all I could think of was the *Psycho* thing.

"Nat?" I said.

"I'm right here," she said, from like two inches away.

I opened my eyes and she was right in front of me in the steam. She was looking at me like I might yell at her, like it might be wrong. Her hair was down and she still had her lipstick on. She put a hand on my chest and then turned her head so I'd hold her against me, and I did.

"I locked the door," she said.

"Good," I said.

There was no candle and no joint. She came to me. The only thing I did was not send her away. It's easy to look back and say you shouldn't of done something. I could lie and say I was just being nice, but I wanted her too. I thought we were close enough to do that. We already loved each other.

It was different in a nice way. I only felt bad about it the next day, when I was with Lamont. But the next night I was fine.

45

Very jealous, but guys are like that. He knew she was my best friend. I never really introduced them but they knew to see each other. He'd wave to her when he pulled in at break; at the most he'd say hey. I told him that she was nice, that in a lot of ways she was like me. He thought she looked silly on her roller skates.

"How old is she anyway?" he said.

"I don't know," I said, though I knew everything about her now—the way her baby toe overlapped, how her hip bones poked out when she laid straight back.

"If you're her friend you should tell her how stupid she looks."

"We're wearing the exact same thing," I said.

He still thought she looked silly on her skates.

I didn't. I liked to watch her glide down the island between the cars with a tray of Volcano Burgers balanced on her fingertips. I liked the way her skirt whipped around her thighs. With her skates on she was taller than me; they made her legs seem even longer. She shaved every three days, and her skin was smooth against my cheek. She didn't look silly to me at all.

"And all that gold of hers," he said, "it's all plated."

"Forget about *her*," I said. "Concentrate on me. We've only got fifteen minutes."

When I came in from break, Natalie took me into the storeroom and kissed me hard against the boxes. Her mouth tasted like peppermint from the swirls that came in the kids' Wacky Packs. When I went to hold her, she twisted away and glided to the door.

"I don't forget *you*," she said.

"What?"

"Making cracks about how I look. I heard the whole thing. Oh Lammy, oh baby, oh Lammy."

"He's my husband," I said.

"You think that makes it any easier for me?"

"Then don't listen."

"How can you be so mean?" she said. "This isn't some stranger you're talking to, this is me."

"What do you want me to do?"

"Like you don't know," she said, and skated away.

We made up later, under the hot water. Her hair turned black when it was wet. It had only been two months, but she knew me completely. The water poured over her belly. She drew a heart in the fog on the mirror. When we came out, Emily looked away. It was like that there, nobody said a word about it.

"What's this?" Lamont said the next day, pointing to a bruise on my thigh. Inside it you could see tooth marks.

"You don't remember?" I said. "You gave me that yesterday."

It was like living a double life, kind of like the writer guy in *The Dark Half*. Natalie wanted me to be hers, Lamont expected me to be his. The one who really needed me was Gainey, and between them I didn't have time for him. While I was in Clara Waters, it was easy, but I only had a few weeks left. Once I got out, I thought, everything was going to change.

46

I got out October 12th, 1985. Lamont took the day off to be with me. He picked me up at the front gate with Gainey in the back. They didn't give me a ten-dollar bill or any of that stuff, I just signed some papers and that was it. Nobody even walked me out.

Natalie had already gone to work on the van. We said good-bye in the room. We'd had a bad night. We both said some things because I was leaving, and she ended up locking herself in the bathroom. Now we were just sorry we'd wasted that time. I told her I'd try to visit.

"That's okay," she said. "I don't expect you to."

"I *will* try," I said.

She started crying. "I've got to go."

"Tuesday," I promised. "I'll come by for a Frito Pie and a lemon Coke, okay? You can take your break with me."

It made her happy but she was still sniffling. I got her a tissue. She used it and gave it back to me at the door.

"I guess I'll see you," she said.

"Tuesday."

"Okay," she said, and kissed me on the cheek, and holding

her with my lips against her neck, I breathed in the smell of her hair. Later I'd steal the shampoo just to keep something of hers.

Below in the courtyard, the van started up, and Natalie turned away from me. I watched her down the stairs. At the door, she waved. When it merged onto 35, she was still looking at me through the window. I waved until the van disappeared. Over the trees I could just see the skeleton of the Ferris wheel, stopped for once. I lit a cigarette and stood at the rail until it was gone, then I went back inside and packed my things.

My first day out was strange. I kept thinking I had to be back at sunset.

Lamont took me straight home. The air conditioning wasn't as strong as Clara Waters. He'd vacuumed and gone food shopping, and Gainey had a new outfit on. I smelled Gainey's neck, and it was sweet, and I swore I'd never leave him again.

"Looks like you don't need me around here," I said.

"There's laundry, if you're looking for something to do," Lamont said.

He put Gainey in the pen with his lovey and pulled me over to the bed. He'd lost some weight, I hadn't noticed in the Roadrunner; you could see his ribs. He was too rough, he didn't know when he was hurting me. I thought of the water, the way Natalie's body mirrored mine.

"Oh baby," he said, "oh come on, baby doll, make your big dog bark."

"What's so funny?" he said.

"I'm just so happy," I said.

"You interested in some brand-new Chunky Monkey?" he asked.

"You know me," I said, "I'm always interested."

In Clara Waters they tested you, so I hadn't done anything in six months. My skin shivered when he flicked his lighter. He tapped it and put it in me. I could feel it heating in my veins like neon. The rush came through me like wind from a semi. It was like slam-shifting gears. It was like being the hood ornament on a runaway truck.

"Whoa," I said.

"I got this new guy," Lamont said. He was sitting next to me, tying off with one of my knee-highs. "He says he can get me as much of this as I can handle."

"You ought to. This is primo stuff."

"Yeah, except he won't front it to me. I'd have to float a loan."

"You know anybody like that?" I said.

He went quiet to enjoy the rush, and I laid back on the bed and thought of Natalie at work, sailing across the lot. He rolled over and his hands ran cold up my legs. It still worked, I thought, but I wasn't sure if that was good. In the middle of it, I grabbed his hair like Natalie did to me and showed him how I liked it.

"I guess you're glad to be home, huh?" he said when we were smoking. He put the cold ashtray on my chest for a joke.

"You don't know," I said.

In the corner, Gainey started to cry and I lifted him out of the pen. He wanted his bottle.

"Guess I'll have to shower all by myself," Lamont said.

"Go ahead," I said, and put my robe on.

I set Gainey in his chair and sort of half watched him, looking around the living room. All the furniture was the same, the TV, the drapes. It was like I never left.

I stuck my head into the bathroom. Even with the fan on, the steam was forming drops on the ceiling.

"Lammy," I said.

"What?" he said behind the curtain.

"Can I take the car on Tuesday?"

"Hey," he said, "you're a free woman, you can do what you want."

47

I was seeing Natalie once a week, more if I could get the car to go shopping on Fridays. It was still warm enough to wear just a skirt and a top. I didn't like having Gainey there. He was buckled into his car seat and couldn't see us.

Natalie was silly. She'd bring out a can of Reddi Wip and a bunch of cherries, or a dish of butterscotch sauce. It got so I brought a towel to be careful of the seats. She liked playing games. I remember the first time she showed me one of her toys. The rubber was shiny like the handgrips on a kid's bicycle, not completely hard. It was way bigger than Lamont.

"What are you going to do with that?" I said.

"What would you like me to do with it?"

"Put it away," I said.

"You're not afraid of it, are you? Watch." She made the whole thing disappear. "See? It's easy. You try."

"I don't think so."

"Don't be such a stiff, Marjorie. It's just fun."

"I'm sorry I'm no fun," I said.

"You sure aren't today," she said, and fit it back into her and started hauling her underwear on.

"I'll try it," I said.

"Forget it."

"Nat."

She fastened her bra and put her top on and snapped the snaps of her skirt.

"Don't go," I said.

"Why?" she said. "Why shouldn't I?"

"Because I love you," I said.

"Right. Once a week for fifteen minutes, twice if I'm lucky. In two weeks I'm not going to have a place to live. Have you even *mentioned* it to him yet?"

"Yes," I said, though I hadn't. I was still building up to it.

"What did you tell him?"

"I told him you might need a place to stay."

"What did he say?"

"Not much," I said.

"So you haven't actually *asked* him."

"I'm going to."

"When?" she said.

"Soon."

"I can't believe you," she said. "You're so full of it." She flipped the front seat up so it hit the horn, and Gainey woke up crying. Wind poured in the door. She got out and turned around and stuck her head in and pointed a finger at me. "You've got to figure out what you want," she said, then slammed the door and skated away.

When I got home, Lamont was already there. I could hear him in the bedroom doing something.

"Hey," I called, to make sure it wasn't a burglar. Casa Mia had had a bunch of break-ins; the cops thought it was one guy.

"Hey," Lamont called back.

I got Gainey settled on the floor with his tool bench and his hammer and went in to see what Lamont was up to. I was trying to come up with a way to ask him about Natalie coming to stay with us until she got on her feet.

He was sitting on the floor on the far side of the bed with his back to me, messing with something.

"You're home early," I said. "Did something happen at work?"

"I didn't go," he said, and I thought something was wrong.

I came around the bed to him and saw the gym bag and all

the packets of twenty-dollar bills. They slapped together as he fit them back in.

He smiled like Jack Nicholson. "I'm taking the day off."

48

Natalie moved in with us around Veterans Day. She slept in the living room. The couch pulled out. I was surprised how much stuff she had. It turned out her landlord had stored it for her even though she'd written him a bad check. Things were like that with Natalie, she could make you do things you didn't want to, things you never thought of before.

Lamont didn't want her to stay with us at first because of his business. The less people the better, he said. He didn't trust her like I did—stupid me. But she had a lot of friends over at Oklahoma Baptist who could move the stuff; he liked that.

She'd never done crank before, she was more the coke type. I started her with a few lines in the mornings. She said the first time Lamont hit her she came, which I think was probably true. He liked doing her up, I could tell from the way he held her arm. It was a power thing with him. It always turns out that way with guys.

We were getting along all right, which was amazing. Natalie could cook, and Lamont liked that. Sometimes Natalie was jealous of Lamont but at least now she stopped asking me to leave him. When Gainey went down for his nap we—

Excuse me a second.

Who is it?

No, tell him to call back later—*of course* **I'll take it.**

I've got to cut you off for a minute, Mr. Jefferies is on the phone. If it's my stay, are you still going to write the book? I hope so. Gainey can use that movie money.

I'm back. No news—the Tenth Circuit Court is still looking at our appeal. Mr. Jefferies says they're staying late just to work on it. There are three judges, two men and a woman. He thinks one of the guys is on our side and trying to turn one of the others around. They're in Denver, an hour behind us. I hope they don't forget that.

You've got to love Mr. Jefferies. He asked if I was finished with this yet.

"I'm trying," I said. "It's long."

"You don't finish, you don't get paid."

I didn't even know I was getting paid, I said.

"No," he said, "you've already *been* paid. It's part of the contract. How many questions have you got done?"

"I'm on number forty-eight," I said. "How many are there?"

"A hundred and fourteen. But the ones at the end are quick. They're all about the murders, all the little details, like what you ordered, who sat in the front."

"Natalie sat in front."

"Whatever," he said. "That's how quick you need to answer them. He wants those the most."

"What time is it?"

"Ten twenty-five."

"I've still got to see Sister Perpetua," I said. "I want at least fifteen minutes with her."

"You better get going then."

"Hey," I said, "are you coming out?"

"Only the sister's allowed to see you."

"I know. I'd still like to see you—just to wave, you know, say goodbye face to face."

"Marjorie," he said, all serious like, "don't give up yet. Just answer those questions. I'll call you when they give me their decision."

Now, is that slick? He didn't answer my question and by the time the decision comes down he won't be able to make it out here in time. And on top of that he's trying to be inspirational. I still don't see how we lost the case.

Here are the three appeals that have worked the most over the years: insanity, mistaken identity and insufficient counsel. Mistaken identity is the best. You always see it on TV, these old black guys who've been in prison twenty years. They're always crying they're so happy. You never hear what happens to the insufficient counsel ones; they probably get tried and convicted again. The insane ones disappear for a little and then come back and do it again. Ours isn't any of the big three. We just say I didn't do it.

What I was saying about Natalie living with us is that she helped out. She'd babysit Gainey when Lamont and me wanted to go out alone. She wasn't freeloading, she paid her way. She'd moved from Coit's to Moxie's Hamburger Heaven, where all the carhops roller-skated and they paid twice as much. More important, she helped Lamont with the west side of town. He was having trouble finding people he could trust, and she set him up with some guys who knew her ex-boyfriend. Without her, we couldn't have paid the loan back on time, and if we didn't pay that one back, we couldn't get the next one, which was even bigger. It was like any drug, you always wanted more.

We got to be with each other every afternoon for a few hours. She had a whole backpack full of toys, and I started getting into them. She was right, it was fun. Some you could put on with straps. The first time I did it with her that way I started laughing.

"What are you doing?" she said. "Don't stop."

"This is hard."

"You want me to put it on?"

"You're better at it."

"You know why," she said. "Because I took the time to learn."

Every day it was something new. We'd put the chain on the door and pull the couch out. At four, we'd take a shower and wake Gainey up and start getting supper together. Everything was ready when Lamont walked in the door.

He'd give me a kiss and take Gainey from me. They'd gotten close while I was away.

"What's cooking there, Natalie?" he'd say, and grab a Tecate from the fridge, and we'd sit down like any other family to eat. This went on for a while; we were just marking the days off, waiting for the big loan to come through. Finally it did. The next day—it was around Thanksgiving—Lamont came home and went into the kitchen and called her Nat, and I knew we'd be all right.

49

In Natalie's book Lamont goes out to the lot of the Wal-Mart that night and brings the money back in a briefcase. I remember reading that and going, "I don't think so."

It was the next morning in some motel room over by Tinker Air Force Base and it was a typewriter case. You needed both hands to carry it. Nothing's heavier than money. Lamont put the chain on and had us sit down on the couch. He opened it on the coffee table. The ink had a strong smell, like bug spray, or drying paint. Put a dollar under your nose, that's what the whole room smelled like. When I worked the counter at Bionic Burger, my fingers smelled like that all the time. Lamont wouldn't let us touch it until he'd counted it twice. Natalie picked up three packets and started juggling.

"Okay," he said, "that's enough," and gathered it up and locked the case again. "Where should we hide it?"

"The bedroom closet," I said.

"That's the first place they'll look."

"The bathroom," Natalie said. "Under the sink."

"That's the second place."

"It's too big for the freezer," I said, and thought of all the places I had my pints. This was way bigger though, more like a pair of half gallons. It wouldn't fit into the couch springs or shoved into my old Nikes at the back of the closet. You couldn't just stick it in a taped-up box of rice.

We split up, going through the apartment like we were agents searching the place. I went into the kitchen and looked under the sink, in the broiler, even in the microwave. I checked the breadbox on top of the fridge, the freezer, the crisper. I opened all the cupboards, top and bottom. I checked our big soup pot and peeked in the slots of the toaster. I started going through the food, ignoring the boxes I was already using. There was nothing big enough really. There wasn't room in the silverware drawer, and the bottom ones were full of old ice trays and place mats, things we didn't use. Where the counter turned, there was this lazy Susan we kept the cereal on. I didn't even have to spin it around; right in front were two family-size boxes of Lamont's Cap'n Crunch.

In her book, Natalie makes it sound like the stupidest place in the world to hide nine thousand dollars. She makes it into a joke on me. She says her and Lamont knew all about my pints, they just didn't want to get into it with me right then. She says they weren't sure about the Cap'n Crunch from the beginning.

They didn't say a thing about it at the time though. They

heard me and came into the kitchen from the other rooms and laughed at the boxes.

"What do you think?" I said.

Lamont picked one up and looked into the mouth of it, then held them together.

"Sure," he said, and smiled so he showed his fangs. "It'll fit."

50

No, but Lamont almost caught us once. It was that last week before we had to leave the city. Natalie had switched shifts, so we only had the mornings together. We were doing things I'd never done with anyone before. It made you feel new, like you'd changed or won something big.

I was tied up facedown, blindfolded with this choke collar on. It was like the beginning of *Gerald's Game;* I love that part. Natalie had her backpack next to the bed. She was pulling things out at random and making me name them.

"The blue one," I said. "The curved thingy. The one with all the knobs."

She jerked the collar and lifted me off the bed.

"Who do you love?" she said.

"You," I said.

"Why?"

I hesitated so she could yank the chain.

"Because you're the best."

"Louder," she said, and when I went to shout, she jerked the chain tight. She let me cough it out before starting again. She reached underneath and lifted me up on my knees. "This might hurt a little," she said, "so just relax."

It was the double one, I could feel the ridges like veins. The top one pinched a little and I let out a grunt. She jerked the chain and pushed.

"Tell me it," she said.

"I love you," I said, but it came out a groan.

Just then a set of keys jingled in the hall. It stopped us. Natalie's breath was warm on my neck.

A key crunched in the lock.

Natalie popped out of me and tore at the bra knotted around my ankle.

The door opened and caught on the chain.

"Open up," Lamont called. "It's me."

Natalie ripped my blindfold off and started on my wrists. The double wiggled like a dog's. She got me free and I threw a robe on while she slipped into the bathroom with the backpack.

Lamont banged the door.

"Just a minute!" I called. Natalie had the bathroom door closed and the water going. On the way through the living room I took a look in the mirror. I closed my robe to hide the collar marks. I'd say the lines on my face were just from being asleep.

"What do you guys do," Lamont said, "sleep all day?"

"Shush," I said. "You're going to wake up Gainey. He's been a bear all morning."

"Nat just getting up?"

"She's been up," I said. "She's making herself beautiful for work."

He'd forgotten an article from *Muscle Car Monthly* on restoring the doors on old Cougars. The guys at the shop were thinking of buying one from Texas. He poked around the living room until he found it. At the door he gave me a kiss and a squeeze through my robe.

"I love you," he said.

And I said, "I love you too."

I put the chain on the door and looked out the peephole.

When I knocked on the bathroom door, Natalie unlocked it. She'd taken the double off and was washing it in the sink. You could see the lines the straps left.

"Come on," I said. "He's gone."

"No," she said, like the moment was over. I kissed her but she held me off. "I've got to get ready for work."

"Nat," I whined.

"I know. But we don't have time to do it right. We'll have all morning tomorrow."

"Promise," I said, and she did, but that didn't help me now. When she was gone I took her backpack into the bedroom and threw the covers off.

She liked scaring me. We'd be fixing dinner with him right in the living room playing with Gainey, and she'd slip her hand up under my skirt or kiss me. Once she stuck her fingers in me while I was brushing my teeth. All I could do was give her a look.

I don't think he suspected, because right then we—Lamont and me—were getting closer that way. I don't know if it was guilt or him getting off on the deal or just me being fired up from Natalie, but we started doing new things too. I pretended they were completely new to me. I even said no a few times before giving in. It was strange; he was more fun now, he was better. It was like being with Natalie made being with him easier.

51

No, my mom never met her. Natalie spoke to her on the phone, but just to answer it and get me. My mom didn't understand why she was living with us.

"She's a friend," I said.

"Of whose?" my mom said, and when I didn't answer, she said, "I'm just asking."

The fact that Natalie had been in prison worried her.

"Hey, remember me?" I said. "I was there too."

"And I'm sure her mother's worried."

"They don't talk."

"Why not?" she said, like it was all Natalie's fault.

"They don't have the greatest relationship," I said. "Not like us."

52

Every other week. Either I took the Roadrunner over to Kickingbird Circle or she came and picked me up outside. She'd bought a Grand Safari wagon even though she didn't have anything to haul around in it. We were getting along because Lamont had taken Gainey to see her a lot while I was away. Gainey still couldn't speak, but whenever he saw her, he lunged for her front. She never apologized for the accident, and she never talked about me being arrested. It was like we just hadn't seen each other in a while.

But it was like that before too. Sometimes I'd think she might change, but she never did, she just listened to the radio and did her gardening and picked up the Popsicle wrappers the kids dropped out front. Every time I came home, the pictures on the mantel were the same, in the exact same places. You knew they moved because she dusted but that was about it. I'd always be that little girl on the tricycle. My father would always be kneeling beside Jody-Jo. She'd always hate me for turning into the person I was instead of going off to college and becoming someone smart who could talk to her about politics and those English detective shows.

But every time I came home I thought things might be different. It only took a few minutes to find out I was wrong. "You're not going to the mall in that," she'd ask, or "Don't you think it might be better to buy him one with an elastic waistband?" When it came to real things, we barely talked anymore. "Well, I can't tell you what to do," she'd say, and I'd make a joke, and she'd misunderstand and say something mean and we'd ride along in silence. Driving home, I'd smoke up a storm. It was just a waste of time.

53

Lamont was supposed to meet with the guy on Friday. I honestly don't remember his name. They were going to meet at the Wagon Wheel Motel in Bethany sometime during the day. It was on Route 66 too. It had a sign shaped like a covered wagon; at night the neon made the wheels move. Lamont would have the money in the Cap'n Crunch boxes in a brown bag like he'd just bought them at Albertson's. He'd planned the whole trip there and back on the map even though it was only like twenty minutes.

At home we'd step on the stuff—just a touch—then weigh it out. We were going to try not to party. Natalie had a bunch of buyers lined up. Saturday she and Lamont would go over to Oklahoma Baptist and get rid of almost half of it. The rest of the people involved Lamont knew from work. Everything had already been set up face to face, no phone calls. By Monday night we'd be done with it. Tuesday we'd pay the loan off and still have three thousand of our own free and clear.

I remember all week Lamont wouldn't get high, not even a single Miller. In bed I tried to distract him but he couldn't relax. Later he'd wake me up with his twitching, and in the morning we were tired. You could see him thinking about it while he ate his

Cap'n Crunch, his eyes bouncing around the kitchen, figuring out what could go wrong.

"Is all of this worth it?" I asked him.

"I don't know what you're complaining about," he said. "You don't have to do anything."

"No," I said, "I just have to live with you."

We both apologized later, but the apartment was like that for a while. You didn't want to be there. Even Natalie got weird about me drinking *her* orange juice. Tuesday we had a fight and instead of making love we sat on the couch watching "Let's Make a Deal." Neither of us even laughed when it came on. Lamont got home late; he'd cut his thumb and had to get stitches. At supper I had to cut his enchiladas. "That's good enough," he said, and waved my hand away. When my mom called to see if I wanted to go Christmas shopping at the mall on Thursday, I was like, yes, get me out of here.

54

Everything happened Thursday.

We got up like usual—first me, to take care of Gainey, then Lamont, so he could use the shower first. Natalie made breakfast in her terry-cloth thingy—huevos rancheros; she was on this Mexican kick. We didn't say anything about tomorrow being the big day. It was quiet, which wasn't like us. Usually we'd at least fight.

Lamont took the Roadrunner and left me the car seat. He wanted to get the engine tuned up for tomorrow. Natalie and me didn't do anything. She left for work early, and barely kissed me. It was like there wasn't room for anything else in our minds.

I changed Gainey and waited for my mom to pull up out front in the Grand Safari. She wouldn't even come in, all she did was honk. It was a little cool because I remember putting a hooded sweatshirt on Gainey. I dropped my keys while I was locking the door, and when I bent down to pick them up I bumped the side of Gainey's head on the knob. He let loose right in my ear, and all the way outside I was apologizing and kissing his boo-boo.

"Crocodile tears?" my mom said. She had a dress on, and gold braid earrings, and I felt bad that I was in my jeans.

"I wish," I said, clicking Gainey in. The part that buckled was crusted with something pink, and I thought, there's just one more thing.

"So," my mom said, "any big plans for the weekend?"

"Nope," I said. "How about you?"

She was hoping we could look for a blazer for Gainey. Navy, maybe green, she said. Something Christmasy. It was a big mission for her, like he'd be missing out on something if he didn't have one. She knew all about them. You couldn't trust their sizes; it was something he'd have to try on. At that point I wasn't going to argue with her. It was just good to be out of the house. I figured the odds of her getting in another accident were humongous, but I still made sure I didn't have anything on me. We passed Moxie's with its sign like a bunch of clouds and a burger with angel's wings playing a harp. I pointed for Gainey to look, but it was crowded and I didn't see Natalie gliding beneath the canopy.

Quail Springs was jammed. They were building the North Pole across from the escalators. A security guard in a brown uniform was standing at the top, making me paranoid. We couldn't eat lunch first or Gainey would be covered with stuff, so we went and tried on blazers for about an hour. I looked at the price tag of one and laughed and said we couldn't afford it.

"Don't worry about that," my mom said. "It's going to be a present from his gram."

From then on she didn't let me look at the tags, and after a while I just gave in.

Finally we got a red one from Toddlin' Town. It made Gainey look like a game-show host. I stood there while my mom paid with plastic, and outside I thanked her.

"Don't force it," she said, then stopped and sighed. "I do appreciate it though."

It was like an apology. Neither of us knew what to say. We stood there with the rest of the shoppers streaming past us, like a wreck on the interstate.

"Now," she said, "where should we eat?"

We had Chick-Fil-A. While we were eating I noticed a knot behind Gainey's ear. My mom parted his hair to check it out.

"He'll be fine," she said. "They're tough."

We looked through the Evelyn & Crabtree and the Laura Ashley store and bought Gainey a cookie from the lady with the cart. The blood pressure mobile was out in the lot with KOMA, and the Heart Association was giving out balloons. I tied the string around Gainey's wrist. He flapped his arm like he was trying to get rid of it.

"That wasn't such a bad day," my mom said in the car.

"It was good," I said.

Gainey was between us in the front. I was holding his balloon in my lap so she could see. I was still a little paranoid about her driving, so I was helping her.

"You can get over," I said. "You're fine on my side."

"Thank you," she said.

At this point we were just trying to get home before the spell wore off.

We were coming up on Moxie's, the long strip with Jimmy's Egg and La Roca and Arlene's Creamy Whip. In between them were a bunch of old motels with cracked swimming pools and blinking neon arrows. At night the place looked like Vegas; now it just looked sooty.

"Okay," I told Gainey, "look for Aunt Natalie."

It wasn't crowded at all, which made sense, since it was only four-thirty. The right side was empty, but out front there were two or three cars, one of them a pretty rare Corvair—a Corsa convertible. A carhop stiff-armed the door and skated out with a tray, but she was small and dark. I turned to see if Natalie was on the other side of the building, not expecting anything, and there, parked in the farthest spot beneath the canopy, was a yellow Roadrunner.

I twisted in my seat to make sure I was seeing it right—the black stripes and the dog dish hubcaps I'd polished myself, the dual exhausts. There it was, just sitting back by the dumpster, the windows so dark you couldn't see in.

"She there?" my mom said.

"No," I said, trying to sound normal.

"She's probably taking a break. Did I ever tell you I did some waitressing?"

"No."

"Oh," she said, "way back. I think every woman should. It really teaches you a lot about people."

"It does," I said. "It sure does that."

She wouldn't stop talking. I held on to the balloon, wanting to pop it, watching the traffic flash by. She could get in an accident now, it didn't matter to me. I kept seeing the Roadrunner sitting under the canopy, it was stuck in my mind. Already I was trying to come up with excuses for them, like they needed to talk about tomorrow, or one of her buyers fell through. I tried to picture them the way—

What do you want?

Hang on a second.

Yes, I want to see her.

Sorry. Sister Perpetua just checked in at the front gate, so I'm going to have to cut this short. Let me just give you the essentials of what happened next.

So we're driving home and Gainey's asleep. We take the turn onto our street, and right in front of Casa Mia is this cop car. It's just sitting there, there's nobody in it.

"I wonder what that's all about," my mom said.

"Probably nothing," I said, because I just wanted her to leave.

I unbuckled the whole car seat so I wouldn't wake up Gainey. My mom handed me the blazer.

"Sure you can handle all that?" she said.

I thanked her—and I really did this time, even if I was impatient. And she could tell too. She waved as she pulled away. I didn't know it then, but that was the last time I'd see her until my trial.

I had to put Gainey's seat on the ground to get my key out. Inside, I could hear voices upstairs—Mrs. Wertz and some man—and I wondered if they'd raided our apartment, if I should book it out of there right now. It was just one cop car; I was being paranoid. And where was I going to run with a baby in a car seat?

Mrs. Wertz and this big cop were in the hall on our floor. Mrs. Wertz was in her socks. As soon as she saw us, she started walking over to me.

"There you are, Marjorie," she said, and put her arms out like she was going to hug me. I was still holding Gainey, so she grabbed my wrists. "Someone broke into your apartment."

"What?"

"It appears they picked the lock," the cop said, all official.

"I'm sorry," Mrs. Wertz said. "I was here all day and I didn't hear anything."

This whole time I was moving toward the door. The cop finally stood aside.

"They made a bit of a mess," he said. "I'd say it was kids."

From the doorway you could see they'd pulled the couch out. The cushions were thrown around, leaning against things. I put Gainey down and went in. The cop was right behind me.

The stereo was gone, and the TV, even the cable box. There were 8-tracks all over the place, and Lamont's hot-rod magazines. They'd taken Natalie's backpack and emptied it onto the carpet. Mrs. Wertz and the cop were pretending they hadn't seen anything.

In the kitchen the fridge was open, and all the cupboards. Flour and cornmeal covered the floor like sand. In the corner, where the counter turned, sat a mound of Frosted Flakes and Cap'n Crunch. I opened the thin door and turned the lazy Susan, but already I knew the boxes were gone.

"It's senseless," the cop said. "Completely unnecessary."

I put Gainey's bed back together and tucked him in. There was a form to fill out, which I did. I thought the cop would take pictures, but he said they weren't necessary, he'd put everything in his report. Mrs. Wertz loitered around until he left, and then I locked the door and started cleaning up. I jammed Natalie's toys into her backpack and threw Lamont's magazines in the trash. It didn't take as long as I thought.

The beer in the back of the fridge was still cold, so I opened one and sat down on the couch. I could have left right then, I could have just taken Gainey and walked away. I was twenty-one, and though it was confused and probably not good for me, I was in love. With him or her didn't matter. Both, if that's possible. They were my life.

Outside, the day was beginning to fade. The air in the room was going gray. I lit a cigarette and said a few things and then just sat there, waiting for them to come home.

TAPE 2 SIDE A

HELLO, HELLO

All right, let's get this over with. Which one did I just do?

If I'd of known there were this many I would of gone a lot faster at the beginning. I don't think it's fair that I have to spend my last hour on earth answering a bunch of lies. Sister Perpetua doesn't either.

Don't get me wrong, I'm glad to be able to tell my side of the story, and the money's important for Gainey. I'm grateful, honestly. It's just bad timing.

Sister Perpetua says we're all forgiven. Do you believe that? I want to.

Do you even believe in God? Or is that too personal? I figure I'm telling you everything, you can at least answer one question of mine.

Do you know the story "Footprints"? It's a big one here on the Row. Etta Mae has a copy on her wall. It goes like this:

This woman is walking down the beach of Life, and behind her in the sand are two sets of footprints.

"Whose footprints are these?" she says.

And Jesus says, "Those are my footprints, for as long as you live I'll be by your side."

So the woman walks on, and soon a storm of Troubles comes along—drugs and alcohol and adultery and money trouble and sickness. It blinds the woman with despair, but she stumbles on, mile after mile, year after year, and when the storm finally clears, behind her in the sand as far as she can see is one set of footprints.

She thinks Jesus has left her, and she wails and beats her breast and says, "Before, there were two sets of footprints and now there's only one. My Lord and Savior, can you tell me why this is?"

"That's simple," Jesus says. "Since the beginning of your troubles I've been carrying you."

Sometimes when I turn around on that beach there are no footprints at all, just sand.

But I know Jesus won't desert me in my hour of need. I know the sister is right and that God is strong. I won't be forgotten and lost, and I will live forever in the most precious blood of our Lord Jesus Christ, amen.

Everything I'm going to say now is true. I've never told anyone this, not even Mr. Jefferies.

I'm sorry, Mr. Jefferies. You believed in me all these years, and I'll always be grateful for that. May God's blessing be on you.

Please remember that I was another person back then, before I accepted Jesus, and that I repent of everything. But I don't scorn that fallen woman, I can't cast the first stone. A lot of her is still in me.

55

My first thought was that it was just a burglar, probably the one who'd hit Mia Casa a few months back. Then I thought about the guy who'd loaned us the money, because who else knew about it? And sitting there with the light going down, I thought about Natalie, and from there it wasn't far to Lamont, and then the two of them together. I thought of how far they could have gotten by now. I thought of their headlights on in the desert, a jackrabbit scooting through them. And maybe that was a test of faith, because I kept waiting.

In the book I don't know how you'd do this. Waiting isn't very dramatic. But it was to me then. I sat on the couch and smoked my Marlboros until the room went dark.

And you know what? We never found out, not to this day. It could have been anyone. It really could have been kids.

56

Lamont came home first. I'd put the chain on the door out of habit and had to get up and let him in. I could barely walk I was so scared.

"What's up with the lights?" he said, and I held on to him.

"What's wrong?" he said.

I couldn't say it. I let go of him to get my carbon of the cop's report.

"What is it?" he said.

He flipped the lights on; the place was clean except for my ashtray on the coffee table. One of the butts had fallen on the floor, and when I bent over to get the report, I picked it up.

"Where's the TV?" he said. "Where's the stereo? What the heck is going on here?"

Except he didn't say heck. You know what he said.

"Marjorie," he said, *"answer* me."

I held the report out and he ripped it from my hand. He read it and looked at me like I could save him if I said the right thing.

"It's all gone," I said.

"What do you mean it's all gone?" he shouted, and pushed me like I was in his way. I fell over the arm of the couch; the carbon floated down to the floor. He stormed into the kitchen and threw the cupboard door open. The lazy Susan was empty.

"Where the heck is everything?" he said. "What the heck is going on here?"

He came into the living room and dove on top of me. He grabbed my throat in both hands and started shaking me, bouncing my head off the cushions and slapping it when it popped up.

"Where is it?" he shouted.

"I don't know," I cried.

This went on for a while after I blacked out, because when I woke up I was in the kitchen and he was pushing my face into the lazy Susan.

"What did you do?" he was shouting, and slamming the door on my head. I fell back and held on to his legs, and finally he stopped hitting me and held on to the counter.

"Oh heck," he said. "Heck heck heck." He just said it for a while, then he sat down on the floor with me and held me and kissed me and said he was sorry.

"I'm sorry," I said, because I was. I shouldn't have gone out with my mom and left the money there alone. It was like going off and leaving Gainey. I was so dumb; I didn't even think of it.

"It's my fault," he said. "It was my money."

"It was *our* money," I said.

"*Was.*"

My eyebrow was cut and the blood was running into my eye. He wiped at it with his sleeve, then kissed the blood away like tears. He took my hand then and kissed my ring.

"I'm sorry," he said again. He didn't have to. I'd already forgiven him.

"What are we going to do?" I said, which was unfair. The only thing he could say was: "I don't know."

57

I don't think he suspected her at first. It was like me, going from the burglar to the guys who lent us the money—to her, to them. It took a little longer because he was with her when it happened. He didn't really suspect her, he just had to make it look like he did so I wouldn't suspect him.

"Would Natalie do something like this?" he asked me, like I knew her and he didn't.

"You never know what she'll do," I said, then "I don't think so."

"When does she get off work?"

"Around eight, I think," I said, to see if he'd correct me. He didn't.

"You mind if we go over there, just to check?"

"I don't think she'd do this," I said. "I don't think she'd have the guts."

"I just want to make sure," he said, and I wondered if he really was worried, if she'd played both of us, and I thought that that would serve him right.

I woke up Gainey and we buckled the car seat into the Roadrunner. On the way over, Lamont kept banging the steering wheel. He waited for the lights to drop to green, not even looking at me. I just sat there, not saying anything.

"Nine thousand dollars," Lamont said. "Nine, thousand, dollars."

58

She was surprised to see us. She came out before Lamont pushed the button to order. She was smiling like a model, like it was fun to work at Moxie's. It was busy and a little chilly, and she had pink leg warmers over the laces of her skates, and for a second her legs and even her face looked strange to me, like someone I didn't know. I wondered if she was in love with him the way I was. I wanted to hear her lie to my face so I could remember it when I finally got back at her.

She bent down and stuck her head in Lamont's window so you could see down her blouse. "Hey," she said, "this is great. I can put it on my ticket."

I waited for Lamont to tell her, but he just turned to me and asked me what I wanted. I looked at Gainey like he might decide. "A Cherub-burger for him," I said, "no pickles. And a milk." It was automatic, it's what he had for lunch when I came by for break.

"Gabriel-burger's good tonight," she said.

Lamont got a boatload of Halos, what they called their onion rings. She glided off, her skirt whipping.

"Aren't you going to tell her?" I whispered, because I knew they could hear us inside.

"I'm *going* to," he said, like he had a plan.

She came back with our order and fit the tray on the window. She'd given us an extra boat of Halos and three pieces of Temptation pie. Lamont motioned her to come closer, and she bent down. He cupped a hand around his mouth and whispered in her ear, and right then, looking at the two of them so close, I thought that I blamed her more because she knew me better. She knew everything, while I'd lied to him.

She looked at me to see if he was telling the truth, and I nodded. She looked back at Lamont with the same face, like it had been her money.

"Heck," she said, just like him, and then she asked him the same question I did.

"I don't know," Lamont said. "I'm figuring that out."

The Order-Matic squawked for her; she had to go. She pushed off and almost ran into another carhop. You could tell she was going to be useless the rest of the shift. Maybe it *was* love; I didn't want to know.

"Hey," I called, and she stopped and came back. "Aren't you forgetting something?"

She looked in across Lamont, completely innocent.

"Ketchup," I said.

59

The plan was for Lamont to go to the guy and see if we could pay it back a little at a time. He'd ask for another loan to stake us. We had the buyers lined up, it was just a matter of getting them the product. The demand was steady; we'd do the same deal three times, give them the profits, and we'd be even.

"Think they'll go for it?" I asked Natalie after Lamont had gone to work. We were in the shower. I was good, I hadn't let on that I knew yet.

"No way," she said.

60

No, I wanted to tell Natalie first. I kept an eye on Lamont. I called him at work right around break time. I checked his underwear and his pockets and watched his money. I made up errands so I could borrow the car.

She was free to leave but didn't, and I thought that was a bad sign. She was following her heart.

In bed I tried to be a little wilder. I had an advantage; I knew what I was up against. I figured I had to do better than she did, give a little more. Looking back, I'm not even sure it works that way, because at that point I wanted to keep him and not her. I don't know how it works; if I did I'd be a genius.

Little by little I found proof. After our last visit to Moxie's, I spent fifty cents and vacuumed the car, then a few days later in the ashtray there was a little red sword they used to spear their cherries. In bed, he said things I'd never heard before. "Tell me what you'd do for me," he said. "Would you kill for me?"

"Yes," I said, because I didn't want to lose him, "yes, yes," but inside I was like, What are you, nuts?

They still hang people in Washington and Montana. Nowhere else though. The books make it sound like a hard job. It's supposed to snap your neck, not strangle you like you'd think. You have to get the length of the drop right, and the knot, otherwise it'll tear your head off. I don't see a big difference, but I guess it would be embarrassing. I can't imagine it would be that hard though. A lot of people do it at home.

61

I told Natalie while we were making love. It was a couple of days after we found the money gone. We were all still flipped out about it, so we needed each other more that way. As soon as Lamont pulled out of the lot, Natalie put the chain on.

We didn't make love like at the beginning anymore. It was normal now, nothing unusual, and I thought how exciting it must be for them, just starting. It made me hate her. We took off our own clothes and got under the covers because it was chilly, then when we were warm we decided what we'd like. Natalie had her backpack open. She hadn't taken a shower yet and still smelled like sleep and her last shift. I wondered if she'd had Lamont yesterday, because he wasn't there when I called.

She kissed me and dug around in her pack and came up with a bra we used to tie each other up. She took my wrist.

I stopped her and took the bra. "It's my turn."

"You know how I like it when you take charge," she said.

"I know."

I tied her off tight so her knees didn't touch the sheets. I slid the blindfold on, already knotted, then threaded the chain through the choke ring and yanked it like I was starting a lawn mower.

She coughed it out. "Not so hard," she said. "That hurt."

"You're okay," I said, strapping on the double.

"Just relax," I said, and started in.

She gave a cry and tried to hop forward but the restraints kept her in place.

I gave her a little more and made her shout.

"Be careful!" she said.

"I know about you and Lamont," I said, and she stopped moving. She turned her head like she could look at me.

"No."

"Yes," I said, "I know everything," and I felt good then. I felt like I could forgive her from this position.

"Please," she said. "Marjorie."

"Please what?" I said.

62

We left the city because Lamont couldn't get the loan. In fact, they wanted it all back.

This time he went to see the guy at a different motel—the Wig-Wam, over on Hefner. He left just before Natalie got home from Moxie's. At midnight he still wasn't back. The TV was gone, so we sat on the couch in our nightgowns and smoked cigarettes, getting up every two minutes to look out the window. We still hadn't made up from the other day. We wouldn't either. It was the last time I'd make love to her.

It got to be one, one-thirty. I emptied the ashtray into the kitchen trash.

"We should call someone," Natalie said.

"Who are we going to call?"

"I don't know," she said, "somebody."

I called the Wig-Wam. Natalie stood right next to me, listening in.

The graveyard guy had just come on. No, he said, he didn't see a yellow Roadrunner.

We went back to the living room.

"Hey," Natalie said at the window. "I think this might be him."

I ran over to her and looked out. The car bounced over the speed bump and its lights blinded us, but when they leveled out it was him.

We ran downstairs to meet him.

He came limping across the lot and we went out in the cold to help.

"What's wrong?" I said.

He pointed to his mouth and shook his head, then pointed to his feet. He tried to say something but it came out retarded, like he was drunk.

"What did they do to you?" Natalie was saying. She was crying, and I was angry that I wasn't.

Inside, his one shoe was bloody. It left prints. It hurt him to go up the stairs. Finally we got him inside and sat him down on the couch. I went to take his shoe off, but he pushed me away. He did a charade of someone writing and Natalie brought him a pen and a pad.

He pointed to his mouth and wrote: *NOVACAINE.*

We both leaned in to look, but he waved us off.

He wrote: *TOE* and made a scissors with two fingers.

"Oh my God," Natalie said.

"Let's see what it looks like," I said, and he let me take his shoe off. He just wanted to warn us.

When I took it off, blood splashed across the coffee table and dripped onto the carpet.

It was the pinkie toe, it was gone. You could see where they'd chopped through the bone, it was white like a rib or a pig's knuckle.

Lamont grunted to get our attention back. On the pad he'd written: *DON'T TALK. DON'T RUN.*

"Forget that," I said, "we're gone."

63

We didn't bring much—a few bags each, some pillows for the car, a cooler for the ice cream. Gainey's playpen was the biggest thing. I packed the trunk. It hurt Lamont to stand up, so he stayed inside while me and Natalie hauled everything down to the parking lot. We each did a line or two to help us out, a little kick start. It was nearly three when we got going, the lights downtown flashing yellow. Me and Natalie were in the front with Gainey asleep between us. Lamont laid across the back with his foot up.

I'd wrapped it in ice and put an Ace bandage around it to keep down the bleeding. We'd stop at a hospital and get it looked at after we got out of the city. He still couldn't talk or eat anything. When I tried to give him some cough syrup for the codeine in it, it ran down his chin.

Yes, we were armed at this point, though I didn't know it. Lamont had the old Colt under the spare in the trunk. He told us when he got control of his lips back and made Natalie jump out at a roadside table and get it.

"What is *this?*" I said.

"It's a gub," he mumbled.

"I can see that. What's it for?"

"To shoop people with."

64

My first thought was to try my mom's place, because she'd have money, but Lamont said that was the first place they'd look. We shouldn't involve her. We headed across Edmond on Second, and when I saw the Route 66 signs, I thought: Depew. There was nothing up there.

What we wanted from the Closes was money and a place to stay while we figured out what our options were. The city was done for us, and probably the state. Our best bet was to rest, stock up the car and head west. We were all agreed on the direction at least.

It was nothing personal against the Closes, I'll say that again if I haven't already. They weren't singled out, they just happened to be in the wrong place at the wrong time. If they'd given us the money like we asked, I bet they'd be alive today.

65

The Closes were home. They were asleep because it was about five in the morning when we rolled in. Their mailbox was a little barn.

I can't describe the exterior because it was dark. They didn't even keep a chore light on. All I remember is coasting in behind the chicken house so no one would see the car from the road. When I turned out the lights it was like being in the middle of the ocean. The only thing you could see was the end of Lamont's cigarette. When he hit it, the light glowed in his eyes.

"How are you doing?" I asked.

"I'm all right. You said you know these people?"

"I know the house. It's the one I'm always telling you about."

"You weren't telling me," he said. "That must have been Nat."

"That was you," I said.

"Not me. I've got no idea where we are."

"We're in Depew," Natalie said. "It's where she grew up."

"See," Lamont said, "Nat remembers."

66

We didn't bust in. We figured it would be easier to break in quietly while they were still asleep, the way the DEA does. I tried to stop Lamont from walking but he didn't trust me and Natalie to do the job right. I told him we couldn't leave Gainey in the car all by himself.

"Bring him then," Lamont said. "Just make sure he doesn't wake up."

"I'm not taking him anywhere near that gun," I said.

"Then stay here. It's not going to take all three of us."

"Just you and Nat," I said. "That's the way you like it anyway."

"The way *who* likes it?" he said.

"Guys," Natalie said, like we were all friends.

"Shut up," I said.

"*Who* likes it?" Lamont said. He put out his cigarette and closed the ashtray, and I couldn't see him anymore. "If you want to come, then come. I'm not going to sit here and argue with you."

"Just go," I said. "You don't want me and Gainey around anyway."

"Yes he does," Natalie said.

"Did I say anything to you?" I said.

"Don't talk to her like that."

"Why not?" I said, and a hand grabbed my neck.

"Because it's rude," Lamont said. He pushed me, letting go. "Are you going to come or what? I don't have time for this."

"No."

"Fine," he said, and opened the door so the bubble light came on. Natalie helped him out and eased the door closed and the darkness blinded me again. Beside me, Gainey was sleeping. I looked up through the windshield, searching for stars. I wished on the first one I saw. Star light, star bright, I said, first star I see tonight, I wish I may, I wish I might, have the wish I wish tonight.

I wish none of this ever happened.

I wasn't there but I can tell you what happened. The door was open, so they went in. I'd told them where the bedrooms were upstairs. Lamont couldn't go up fast enough, so he gave the gun to Natalie. She woke the Closes up. In court, the prosecutor said they slept in different rooms, so she must have done them one at a time. In her book, Lamont does this, and she's not speeding either, she's just there.

I saw this glow above the chicken house when the lights came on, so I knew they made it inside. I got out of the car and peeked around the corner; there was no one on the porch waving that the coast was clear, but they'd pulled the shades down. I figured it was all right, I hadn't heard any shots.

I say all this like it was normal because it almost was to me. You get in these situations sometimes. You know the whole thing is weird, but you know you can't change it, so you just start thinking that way.

Inside, Lamont and Natalie were standing in the living room. Lamont had the gun pointed at Mr. Close, who was flat on the rope rug on his stomach, his hands stretched over his head. He was fat and had sky-blue pajamas on, and the bottoms of his feet were dirty. Right beside him, Mrs. Close was wearing a pink flannel nightgown with roses all over it; in the back she was almost bald, just a little white fluff of hair. When Lamont saw me with Gainey in the car seat, he tipped his head toward the stairs.

I took Gainey up to my old room and put him on the bed, fencing him in with pillows in case he rolled over. When I came back down, Natalie was tying the Closes to a pair of kitchen chairs with clothesline. Lamont had his foot up on the table and his shoe off. He was cooking up, the flame wrapping around the spoon, and instantly my body wanted it. And I thought, it's going to be a long day.

67

The only things I recognized from my childhood were the woodwork in the living room, the banister and the light at the top of the staircase. There wasn't much left. They'd painted and changed the kitchen cabinets and bought all new appliances. They carpeted the stairs, which I guess old people do. There was a one-piece vinyl shower stall with sliding doors instead of the pink-and-black tile. The piano was gone, and the glider. I kept thinking, it's only been sixteen years.

The biggest change was how small everything seemed, even the yard. It felt a little like a dollhouse, like it wasn't completely real. But then, everything did then.

68

Lamont was going to take Mr. Close into Chandler to use his bank card. The machine had a camera, so they had to take the Closes' car, an ugly old LeSabre. Lamont would drive it to the parking lot of the bank, then they'd switch places. The Closes' checkbook said they had over a thousand dollars in their account; Mr. Close said he could take out three hundred dollars a day. Lamont's idea was to go right before midnight, then wait five minutes and do it again.

The only problem with that was we had to keep an eye on the Closes all day. We moved them into the dining room so we didn't have to look at them all the time, but still I felt we should feed them. In Natalie's book, she makes them tuna melts; it was actually me, and they were pigs-in-a-blanket and crinkle-cut fries. I know it's a little thing, but you should know the truth.

We went through all the closets and dressers. Mr. Close had a bunch of guns. Lamont gave me and Natalie each a pistol and took an old shotgun for himself. In the attic he had some muscle magazines hidden in a trunk, or maybe they were hers. Natalie waved pages in front of them. "Oh Bruno," she said.

There were two calls during the day. We just let them ring. Neither of them called back, which surprised me, and I said so.

"It's probably the same person trying again," Natalie said.

"Duh," I said.

Most of the time I was busy with Gainey. He was good most of the day, gnawing on saltines. I got him down for his nap right on time. I didn't want to mess up his schedule.

Finally it got dark. We were worried someone might see the Roadrunner. Natalie made chimichangas for the Closes, just like the book says, then we watched TV. It was Friday night, I don't remember what was on; you can look it up. I thought we should let the Closes watch too, but Lamont said they were fine in the dining room. I asked if I could at least turn the light on for them.

He took out his pistol and handed it to me. "Why don't you just give them this?"

His foot was better, he said. It had stopped bleeding so much. He didn't think he needed a doctor; Natalie and I did. We didn't have time, he said, and we made him promise he'd see one whenever we got where we were going.

The late news came on, and "M*A*S*H," and Lamont hit himself again. I rolled up my sleeve and laid my arm on the table. Behind me, Natalie waited for hers.

Lamont had to wake up Mr. Close.

"Okay, pardner," he said, "time to hit the dusty trail."

We watched the late movie while Lamont was gone. It was some vampire thing with Christopher Lee and Peter Cushing, *Castle of the Curse* or something. Mrs. Close was awake, so we brought her chair over. I was surprised how light she was.

I couldn't concentrate on the movie. I kept thinking of the thirty-five miles to Chandler and how empty it would be at night. It used to be a cattle town; right outside the limits there was a rotted old loading chute, and that was fifteen years ago. There might be one pickup parked at an angle on Main Street, but nothing open. Most of the storefronts would be for lease. The county farm bureau, a cafe where you could get good biscuits and gravy and a bottomless cup of coffee. It was the kind of place I was afraid I'd end up—not even a stoplight anymore, the lines on the road fading away, one potbellied cop waiting for speeders with out-of-state plates. I pictured him watching the LeSabre turn into the bank's parking lot.

On TV, a Mountain Dew commercial came on, all these kids having fun at some swimming hole.

"You guys have any diet Pepsi?" I asked Mrs. Close. She nodded and I took off the gag so she could tell me where it was.

It was decaf because of Mr. Close's blood pressure, but it was still good.

"You sure you don't want one?" I asked, and not to be mean either.

And I think she knew I was trying to be nice, because she said, "No thank you."

But after a few sips it was disgusting and I put it down.

69

Mr. Close was alive when they came back but he had a big knot above one eye and his teeth were bleeding. Lamont was bleeding too, he had this long brushburn on his forehead. One knee of his jeans was torn and he was breathing hard. He pushed Mr. Close down onto the rug and held the gun under his chin while Natalie tied his elbows behind his back and his ankles together. Mrs. Close was crying.

"Get her out of here," Lamont said, and Natalie started dragging her chair into the dining room. "And shut her up. Who said you could take that off?"

"What happened?" I asked, but he brushed past me into the kitchen and came back with a black garbage bag. The toe made him wobble.

"What is going on?" I said.

He fit the garbage bag over top of Mr. Close and started hitting him with the butt of the gun. I tried to stop him but he pushed me down. He picked up one of those paperweights with the snow in them and hit him with it; it broke and water splashed over the bag. Mr. Close was flat on the rug. One of his hands stuck out of the bag, twitching.

"What are you doing?" I was screaming. I had Lamont's arm but he was too angry. He grabbed a little clock off the mantel and bounced it off of Mr. Close's chest.

"Try and run me down now," Lamont screamed at the bag. He kicked him with his good foot and a stain spread down one leg of Mr. Close's pants. It sounded like he was throwing up in the bag. Lamont wouldn't stop kicking him, and finally Mr. Close stopped making noise and just laid there.

"What happened?" I said, but he pushed past me again. He put a trash bag over Mrs. Close and hit her with the gun so hard that her chair almost tipped over. The gun flew out of his hand and bounced off a hutch. He swore and sucked his knuckles and Natalie picked it up for him.

"What the heck happened?" I shouted. It was infectious; we were all a little crazy now.

Here's what he told me, I don't know if it's the truth. They made it into Chandler okay. They got to the bank and started to do the switch. Somehow Mr. Close got behind the wheel while Lamont was still trying to get around the front of the car, and Mr. Close tried to run him over in the parking lot. He knocked Lamont down but ran into the drive-in window and Lamont hobbled over and put the gun to his head. Lamont didn't know if there were any cameras there. They went through the drive-thru like they planned, except it was after midnight now, so they'd only be able to get three hundred dollars. So Lamont is already mad, and they pull up and put the card in, and the machine's out of money.

So there's your answer to the second part—no, he didn't get any.

70

We didn't sleep because we were up. We packed the Roadrunner
so we could get going early. I made sandwiches for the cooler,
and took two of those blue ice things from the freezer. The ice
cream was soup so I pitched it. The speed seemed minor after
watching Lamont in the living room. I'd seen him that angry
before, but only toward me. It was weird; I almost felt left out.

We didn't do anything with the Closes, we just left them
where they were. I remember taking a break from packing, coming in to get a beer and sitting on the couch to see what the
weather was going to be like tomorrow; when I went to sit down I
had to step over Mr. Close like Jody-Jo when he was asleep or
just wouldn't move. I sat there and flipped through the channels
until I found the weather, then I got up and stepped over him and
went back to packing.

Mrs. Close woke up right when we were about to leave. She
was moaning like she had a stomachache or something.

"Shut her up," Lamont told Natalie.

"It's already on as tight as it can go," she said.

"I don't care *how* you do it," he said, "just do it."

71

Lamont killed the Closes, if you want to get technical about it. He
burned them alive.

Firestarter, right?

That's one way I wouldn't like to die—like Joan of Arc or
those old-time witches. In the movies you can always tell the
flames are like ten feet away from them. In real life I bet it would

take a long time. They'd smell, like when you forget something in the oven. Nobody does it anymore, not officially at least.

So it was Lamont. Natalie didn't kill anybody until the Sonic.

72

When we had everything packed and I'd fed Gainey his breakfast, Lamont brought a gallon can of kerosene up from the basement and told us to get in the car. Outside it was cool but bright, the grass was wet with dew. You could smell the red dirt. Everything had gone too far, and I was trying to concentrate on the little things. I put Gainey up front because it would help with the cops if they stopped us. While I was getting him set, he clawed off an earring. I swore and made him cry, then apologized. I was all buckled in when I remembered his diaper bag.

Inside, Lamont was splashing the kerosene over Mr. Close. It puddled in the folds of the trash bag. His hand was flicking like it was trying to shoo a fly. In the other room, Mrs. Close was moaning, and I hoped Lamont would count that against Natalie.

"Hold up!" I said, and zipped in and grabbed the diaper bag. "Okay," I said, "go ahead."

I followed him into the dining room, where he did Mrs. Close. Her nightgown went gray where it spilled. I noticed the space where the piano was supposed to go and told Lamont about it. When he was done, he threw the can against the hutch, breaking some plates. He took out a pack of matches.

"Can we talk for a minute?" I asked him. "About me and Natalie."

"Why?" he said, and then he saw that I wasn't going to let it go. "Okay," he said, and we sat down on the couch. His brushburn was sweating little beads.

"I'm all done with her," I said. "It's over."

"So?"

"I mean I'm committed to you."

"It's a little late for that, isn't it?"

"Is it?" I said.

"I don't know."

"I love you," I said.

"I know that," he said, "I love you too," but he didn't sound happy about it.

"We should get going," I said. "I just wanted you to know that."

"Okay," he said.

And he kissed me then, I don't know why. I didn't expect it.

I held the front door open while he flicked matches at Mrs. Close. It took him a few tries. Every time a match scratched, she jumped. It made me sad because she was nice, giving me the diet Pepsi and saying thank you.

Mr. Close caught on the first one.

"Did you see that?" Lamont said as we ran across the yard, and for the first time in a while it was like it used to be. But I knew that wouldn't last.

73

Gainey was in the car with Natalie the whole time. The only time he would of seen anything is when I brought him from the kitchen out to the car, and I turned so I was between him and Mr. Close. He won't have nightmares, at least not about that.

The one way that gives me nightmares is the way they used to do it in India. They made you lie down on the ground and brought this trained elephant in to step on your head. It's like the trick with the girl in the circus except the elephant puts his foot down. Sometimes I have this nightmare where I'm dressed up in this sequined outfit like a trapeze artist, and they make me lie down in the sawdust, and the elephant comes out. It's like it's real. I'm lying there looking up at the bottom of his foot. It starts coming down. It's dirty and there are peanut shells stuck to it.

And it doesn't stop. It steps right on my head. I can hear my nose crack and feel everything getting pressed flat. When it's over, I get up and my head's like an all-day sucker on my neck, like in a cartoon. You can see the footprint right in the middle of it. And then the brass band goes ta-daa, and I curtsy and throw my arms out wide like it's a trick.

74

I drove. Lamont's foot still hurt him, and Natalie didn't have any real experience at the wheel. The state police were running brand-new Crown Victorias with a factory interceptor package, and they were still thirty horsepower short of our Hemi. The only thing that was going to catch us was a Harley Electraglide, that or a chopper.

Our plan was to head west, cutting just north of the city. 40 had all the cops. We'd stick with the smaller highways and state roads. East of the state line there were lots of empty stretches where we could make up the time.

We picked out a few places we might try—Bullhead City, Lake Havasu City, Roswell, New Mexico. Natalie suggested Victorville, or Truth or Consequences. Lamont said San Bernardino was the crank capital of the world; the Marines trained right near there at Twentynine Palms.

"Yuma," I said.

"Fresno," Lamont said. He had the atlas open on his lap, his finger following a road through the Texas panhandle, and Natalie was looking over his shoulder, and I couldn't tell if the possibilities for me were opening up or narrowing down. I checked my mirrors and kept the needle right between the 5s.

75

We all planned the Sonic job, all of us. We weren't even off of 66 when we needed gas. We had twelve dollars between us, which wouldn't even fill the tank, so we knew we had to do something.

It was Saturday. At my old Sonic the manager would do a drawer skim right before the lunch rush and deposit it before the bank closed at noon. Friday was our busy night so it was always a chunk of money.

"How much is a chunk?" Natalie said.

"Two thousand?" I said. "It's probably more now."

"That'll do it," Lamont said. "What about alarms?"

"None. No cameras either. It's a real cut-rate operation. Lunch shift you're going to have six people at the most. The manager's trained to hand over everything. The rest of them are just kids."

He didn't answer right away. We were coming into Arcadia, a few miles east of Edmond. We passed Bob's Bar-B-Que and the Round Barn; already there were tourists hanging around outside. I looked at Natalie in the mirror, and she looked back at me like it wasn't her decision.

"What time is it now?" Lamont said.

76

Eleven-ten.

The weather was bright, like I said. Fifty, fifty-five, some high clouds. Light wind. You can make it windy if that makes it more dramatic, red dust blowing all over. Rain would be even better. And you definitely want to make it at night so you get the red neon, that's what Sonic's famous for. Maybe at closing time while they're mopping up, that way we'd take them by surprise.

77

I had on Levi's and a mustard sweatshirt with Snoopy on it, the kind with the pocket in front for your hands. Under that I was wearing a light blue Eskimo Joe's T-shirt. Just a regular bra and underwear, white tube socks, red Chuck Taylors. A pair of fake Ray-Bans. Little heart earrings Lamont had given me for my birthday and my pearl ring. I looked normal.

Lamont was wearing a blue-and-black-plaid flannel shirt, his jeans with the hole in the knee and Mr. Close's work boots because his shoes were ruined. The chain for his wallet was hanging out, and his pocketknife case on his belt. He didn't wear any rings or anything like that. White tube socks with stripes, regular brief-type white underwear.

Natalie had on designer jeans—Guess or Jordache, something dumb. She had on a white pullover with no sleeves that was too small for her; you could see a line of skin right around her belly button. Beige flats and no socks. At least two gold chains, gold hoop earrings, more than one ring on each hand. Probably some kind of barrette, and makeup, definitely coral lipstick. She liked pink or blue bras and underwear, always matching.

Gainey had on a green jumper with a hood and little blue tennis shoes with rainbow laces. Pampers.

Everyone inside except the manager had red-and-black Sonic uniform tops on, and black jeans. Who knows what they had underneath.

78

We weren't heavily armed. Lamont had his pistol and Mr. Close's shotgun, which we didn't even take out of the trunk. Natalie had a .45 and I had a little .22.

I didn't even want the thing. I'd never fired a gun before, I didn't even know how to load it or take the safety off, Lamont had to do that for me. He said we wouldn't have to shoot but if we did we'd better know how.

79

I was driving, Lamont was the passenger, Gainey was in back behind me, and Natalie was in back behind Lamont. This goes for after the robbery too; we kept our positions to avoid confusion.

I'm not going to call it a massacre, like it says on the cover of her book. A massacre is more than five people. She's just using it to sell more copies.

I read somewhere that one of John Grisham's books sold 8 million copies. It's okay, you're still a better writer than he is. Maybe this one will do better.

80

I don't remember what we talked about. Maybe we didn't say anything, maybe just "Turn here," or things to remember once it got started.

It was a simple plan. I wouldn't leave the car. We'd pretend we were reading the menu. We'd wait till all the carhops were inside. Lamont would go in first, then Natalie right behind him. I wanted to go with him but he said we all knew I was the best driver and that he was counting on me. He just said it so I wouldn't be jealous, which was dumb, because I already was. I said fine.

Inside, he'd ask something dumb like could they use the restrooms, and make the manager explain that only employees were allowed in the building. Once Lamont had him away from the phone, he'd show him the gun. Then Natalie would slip in behind the counter and grab the person doing drive-thru. The rest was just rounding up the carhops and the fry cooks and locking them in the walk-in fridge. Clear out the safe and the register and stick it in a sack.

I was supposed to buzz for an order and the number for my stall would light up on the panel so they'd know it was me. Lamont would get on that channel and tell me when to pull around to the window. Natalie would hand me the sack and I'd stick it under Lamont's seat, then roll around and pick them up out front and we'd be off.

I came up with most of the plan because I'd worked there, I have to admit that. I still think it would of worked if it wasn't for Victor Nunez. Maybe someone would of still gotten our license plate, but it wouldn't of been anything like what happened. We didn't go in planning to kill anyone like the prosecution said. So right there is five counts that should of been second degree at the most. At least that's what Mr. Jefferies says.

I don't know what we said to each other, it wasn't anything important. I'm sure you can come up with something more interesting.

81

Whatever it was, we turned it down low before we pulled into the Dairy Kurl to get Gainey his sundae. We'd all been up for two days straight and we needed to think. I don't remember an 8-track. If it was the radio it would have been KATT, the classic rock station, only because there's no good rock station around here. Everything's country or Christian. The Katt played your usual Stones and Zeppelin with a little Aerosmith or the Crue thrown in. It's still like that, kind of stuck in a time warp.

If you want a great driving tune, you might go with "Radar Love," it pretty much tells the whole story. There's a live album with about a sixteen-minute version. There's this great line in it, *The radio's playing some forgotten song.* You can put that in because it's true—I can't remember what was on.

Nothing wimpy though. "Land Speed Record" by Hüsker Dü was one of our favorites, you can always use something off of that. Louder, faster!

82

I guess not everyone's seen a Sonic. I thought they were everywhere.

The one we went to had a drive-thru lane as well as the regular drive-in part. The drive-thru lane wraps around the building. You go behind and there's the order board, then you come around the other side and pick up your food at the window. The drive-in stalls are outside of the lane; there are twenty-four, twelve on each side. Over the stalls you've got a canopy held up by the poles the Order-Matics are on. The ends are red triangles, which is part of the logo. The stalls are kind of diagonal, and they're all oil-stained. You pull up and your window's right by the Order-Matic.

The building itself is square with a red triangle on top. There are two windows in front and each of them has a neon sign — one says *Burgers* in red script, the other says *ONION RINGS* in green block letters. Speakers attached to the canopy play rock all day long, just loud enough so you can hear what song it is. You'd hate to live by the place.

In back there's a regular dumpster and a grease-only dumpster that the sparrows love. In front there's a skinny island of grass and shrubs between the in and out lanes of the drive-thru, with a fake Japanese bridge about a foot high.

The sign's like a gas station sign, it lights up from inside. *SONIC*, it says in red, *America's Drive-In*. You see the other side when you leave; it says, *Happy Eating*. At night red neon completely outlines the canopy and the building. It's a great place to take your car right after you've waxed it. The food's not bad either. Even when I worked there I'd eat it.

Mr. Jefferies has tons of pictures of it. He could even take you there. You'll probably see a lot of little stuff I've forgotten.

It's funny, the post office in Edmond has this fountain outside with the names of all fourteen victims on it. You'd think Sonic would do something like that for its employees, but there's nothing. In Mr. Jefferies' pictures the windows are fixed and the carhops are serving people like nothing ever happened.

83

It wasn't lunch yet so it wasn't busy. There was a new T-bird in a stall on the right, halfway up, and on the left in about the same place an old gold Tempest that Natalie thought was a Goat. She was trying to impress Lamont with her knowledge of cars.

"Close," I said. "It's got the same nose."

"It's not a LeMans?"

"389 tripower," I said, "four-speed, probably has that old Positrac," and Lamont laughed like he was proud of me.

A carhop came out with a tray—Kim Zwillich, the short one with the red ribbon holding her ponytail. I could only see the neon in the windows; the signs were on, even at eleven in the morning. We pulled into the last stall on the right. At the far end of the lot the employees' cars were parked head-in next to the dumpsters. There were four of them, all small and foreign, beat-up little riceburners.

It was cool under the shade of the canopy. Lamont stuck his gun in his belt. Natalie put hers in her purse and left the flap unsnapped. We watched the guy carhop come out to the T-bird with a single drink—Reggie Tyler. He was Natalie's size, with long blond hair parted in the middle and feathered back. We were too far back for me to see if he had a mustache at that point. When he disappeared around the corner, Lamont opened his door.

"Can you get some napkins?" I asked, because Gainey was making a mess.

"Napkins."

"Be careful," I said.

"We will," he said. "You just be ready."

I wanted a kiss but he was already out, with Natalie right

behind him. I watched them walk toward the front under the canopy. Lamont had an extra sway in his step because of the toe. They were talking like nothing was up, so close together you'd swear they were married. I was supposed to look at the menu like I was trying to decide something, and right then I thought, heck, I can do that.

84

They were in there maybe thirty seconds. It could have been shorter or longer, I wasn't counting. The clock on the dash worked, Lamont was always proud of that, but I wasn't timing them. I had my finger over the order button, ready to see if everything was going okay.

Lamont came on. "We're in," he said. "Stand by."

"Standing by," I said.

It was like the astronauts talking.

Lamont left the mike open. "Over there," he was saying to someone. "Shut up and do it."

I heard the register peep and the drawer kick out. Then I heard the shots.

85

I wasn't there for that, so Natalie might be right. I don't know about Victor Nunez overpowering her, because he wasn't that big. He was chubby, one of those kids that jiggles, the kind that gets picked last—not someone who'd surprise you. Mr. Jefferies showed a bunch of diagrams in court, and from where Natalie says she was standing and where the door of the stockroom was, it looks like she just didn't know he was behind her. She'll never admit it though, because that would make it all her fault.

As far as I could tell, this is what happened. Lamont went in first. Everybody was inside, just like we planned. No one was by the phone, so Lamont pulled out his gun. He asked which one of them was the manager, and Donald Anderson said that he was. Lamont went around the counter to get everyone away from the register and the Order-Matic panel. At the same time, Natalie made Margo Styles take off the headset she used to do the drive-thru window. Lamont called me and started on the cash drawer. So far everything was going okay.

This whole time, Victor Nunez was in the stockroom, getting a bunch of cups. When he came out he must of seen Natalie standing there with the gun. It was noisy from the hiss of the grill and the bubbling of the Fry-o-lators, so maybe she didn't hear him. Maybe she was scared and froze up. Whatever. Either Victor Nunez stopped and decided to be a hero or he just reacted, no one knows. But the next thing he did was come up behind Natalie and grab for the gun.

Was there a struggle like in the movies? Did Lamont have to decide whether to risk shooting her, the great love of his life? I have no idea, I wasn't there. Natalie makes it sound like Victor Nunez practically had to break her wrist to get it, but that would of given everyone time to take cover. All I know is I heard a bunch of shots.

I don't know what order they hit everyone in. One hit Reggie Tyler in the ear. One hit the slush machine, because when I got there it was squirting all over the floor. One hit Donald Anderson in the side. One hit Victor Nunez and took most of one cheek away. And one hit Lamont in the ribs.

86

My first reaction was to hope *we* were doing the shooting. I'm sorry but it's true. I hung on to the steering wheel, waiting for the noise to stop.

Lamont swore and there was another shot. "That's what you get," he said.

A girl was crying in the background.

I looked around the lot. The family in the T-bird hadn't heard anything, which I thought was impossible.

"Margie," Natalie called, "get in here."

I looked in my purse to make sure the gun was still there. Gainey had chocolate sauce all over his chin.

"Mama'll be right back," I said.

I wondered if I should lock the doors or not. I left them open in case we had to move fast.

While I was walking along the side of the building, another car pulled in, a new Camaro convertible with a blonde in it, so blond her hair was almost white. She passed me and curled around the other side. I turned the corner in time to see the guy in the Tempest check her out. There were two doors, one to go in on the right, the out one on the left. They both had a sticker that said *EMPLOYEES ONLY*. I opened the in door and went in like I was just late for work.

87

The first thing I saw was Lamont holding his ribs. His shirt was soaked, and the hip of his jeans below it. He was next to the register, holding his gun on everyone. Natalie stood by the drink machine, holding hers out the same way.

They were all on the floor between the grill and the Fry-o-lators. A cloud of greasy smoke hung under the lights; the whole place reeked of meat. There was no music inside. Victor Nunez and Reggie Tyler were on the floor, but they were dead and you could tell. A piece of Victor's face stuck to the soft ice cream machine; his red visor lay on the grill, cooking. Reggie's legs were under him at a funny angle. The floor was tile and had a drain, and the blood was running into it. Kim Zwillich and Margo Styles were clutching each other. I forgot to take out my gun. I just stood there looking at everything. A Coke clock went around on the wall.

"He says the safe's not open," Lamont said, poking his gun at Donald Anderson. He was sitting in front of the others like he could protect them. He had a tic in his right eye, and his lip was starting to follow. He had on a white alligator shirt with the Sonic triangle over the heart while the rest of them had cheap red ones that buttoned up with a patch that said *Sonic* like it was a gas station.

"He can open it," I said. "He's got the combination."

"I don't have it," Donald Anderson pleaded. "I just started working this week."

"Get over there," Lamont said.

"I don't have it!"

Lamont took a step and Donald Anderson crawled toward the corner. His knees left trails in the blood.

Natalie swore and Kim Zwillich and Margo Styles huddled closer.

Over the Order-Matic, a woman said, "I need a number three and a rainbow slush with a dash of vanilla."

Lamont looked at Donald Anderson, then looked at me.

"Did you get that?" the woman said. It had to be the blonde in the Camaro, at least I hoped so.

I stepped over a fallen stack of cups and punched the button for stall 17.

"Yes, ma'am," I said. "Is that with or without fries?"

"With."

"Large or small?"

"Large."

"What would you like on that three?"

"Everything please."

"What size slush—small, medium or large?"

"Large, and I'd like just a dash of vanilla ice cream on top."

"Okay," I said, and rang it up like a regular order. "That's a number three with everything, large fry, large rainbow with vanilla. Will there be anything else?"

"That's it," she said.

I totaled it. "That'll be three forty-four. We'll have your order out to you in a jiff. Thanks for cruising Sonic."

Behind me in the corner, Donald Anderson was working at the combination. Lamont had the gun on him, jabbing him in the back of the head with the barrel.

"Who else would know it?" Lamont said.

"He knows it," I said. "The manager handles all the money."

Outside, the family in the T-bird were leaving. The guy in the Tempest had a book open.

The Order-Matic let out a blast of static. "Excuse me," the blonde said, "can I get that number three without tomatoes?"

"No tomatoes on that three," I said, like I was saying it to someone. "No problem, ma'am."

"Thank you."

"Bring one of them over here," Lamont called, and Natalie grabbed Kim Zwillich by the arm and broke her away from

Margo Styles. Victor Nunez and Reggie Tyler just laid there, draining.

"How long is this going to take?" I said. "Should I get this lady's order?"

"Can you get it?" Lamont said.

"I can try," I said.

Not all the burgers on the grill were burnt. I fixed a number three, got a large fry from under the heat lamp and ran a rainbow slush. The machine dribbled cause it had been hit; I was afraid there wouldn't be enough, but there was. I tried not to look at the ice cream machine. I put the lid on and got the straw and the napkins. When the tray was ready I set it on the counter.

"Take your shirt off," I told Margo Styles, and she did.

It was warm, the armpits sopping. The headband of her visor was damp. I took her change apron and fastened the strap behind my back. It wasn't until I was outside that I remembered the no tomato.

"That's all right," the blonde in the Camaro said. "I can pick them off."

It was a beautiful car, I said, and she told me how she liked it, what it could do. I could feel the guy in the Tempest watching us. I thought how I'd like to get in and just go, hit the interstate and just motor.

I made change and started walking away when she called, "What about those little candies, don't I get one?"

Heading for the door, I saw my shoes had left bloody prints on the walk.

When I went back inside, the bodies were gone, just a big smear of blood on the tiles, the lines left by their heels. Natalie was herding Margo Styles toward the back with a big kitchen knife in one hand and the gun in the other. Margo Styles was crawling on her hands and knees and Natalie was kicking her. Lamont and Donald Anderson were still working on the safe;

Donald Anderson was sobbing and bleeding from one ear. Beside them, Kim Zwillich was lying on the floor with her eyes closed and blood all over her front. The tip of one of her fingers lay on the floor like a dropped Tater Tot.

"How's it going?" I said.

"It's not," Lamont said. "He says he can't remember it. I'm beginning to think he really doesn't."

"He's scared."

"And I'm not," Lamont said.

From the back came a scream, then pleading, then another scream. Everything on the grill was smoking now. I grabbed a handful of peppermints and checked the clock.

"Three more minutes," I said. "It's coming up on lunchtime."

In the back Margo Styles was screaming. It was good to get outside in the fresh air.

"Thank you," the blonde said.

"You're very welcome, ma'am," I said. "It sure is a beautiful car."

I looked around the other corner to make sure the Roadrunner was okay, and it was. A yellow Coronet pulled in, and right behind it a Ranchero with a pinball machine in back.

"Forget it," I told Lamont. "We've got to get going." In a way, it wasn't really me; it was the speed and the situation. Everything was just clicking. It was like work, I was just doing what I had to do.

Lamont hauled Donald Anderson up from his knees. "Get her," he told me, so I did.

I'd like to apologize to the Zwillich family for what I'm going to say next, even though I know they heard some of it at the trial.

I couldn't lift her so I dragged her by her wrists. Her hands were all chopped up. She was missing two fingers, and there were cuts on the backs that were still bleeding. In the middle of dragging her past the grill, her eyes opened. She was already slippery and she started fighting me, twisting out of my grip. I grabbed the first thing I could find—a metal spatula—and hit her across the face with it. I got a good grip again and hauled her through the mess and past the ice machine. Up front, the Order-Matic came on, some lady saying, "I'd like a Supersonic with cheese, onion, mayo, and that's it." Another guy said, "I need a corn dog and a medium Dr Pepper." While I was dragging Kim Zwillich back toward the freezer, I tried to keep the orders separate in my mind, because I thought I'd have to stall them. It was easier that way, having something to think about. God knows what Natalie and Lamont were thinking.

88

I'm not sure if it was Lamont's idea or Natalie's. It wasn't mine. I've worked in enough restaurants to be afraid of getting trapped in one of those things. I'd never do that to someone else.

Part of it was because of the noise, I guess, that and they'd be harder to find.

We didn't use the walk-in fridge because it was full of lettuce crates and boxes of cheese and gallon jars of mayo and pickles; there wasn't enough room for all five of them.

In the freezer they kept long white boxes of burgers with the Sonic logo on them, and chicken patties. The whole thing was no bigger than the cell I'm in right now. If you touched the walls, your finger would stick to the metal for a second and leave a print. There were steel racks on both sides of a center aisle; on the racks were those plastic baskets strawberries come in, except they were filled with Tater Tots. You had to count out just the right number. When someone ordered them, you'd just dump a basket in the Fry-o-lator.

They went in in this order: first Victor Nunez and Reggie

Tyler, then Margo Styles, then Donald Anderson, and finally Kim Zwillich. The only one fully conscious was Donald Anderson, and he was crying. Margo Styles had passed out from the cuts on her front. Kim Zwillich was mumbling something, a prayer or maybe just gibberish.

"Put that away," Lamont told Natalie, and she threw the knife across the room into a sink. Her one fist looked like she'd dipped it in a bucket of red paint. Her eyes were dilated, just a ring of color left, like the sun during an eclipse, and I looked at her and I thought, how did she keep from getting it all over her?

89

I didn't stab any of them. I didn't have the knife. And I didn't have the time to stab Margo Styles eighty-nine times. I was taking care of everything else.

Part of why I might die tonight is the eighty-nine times. I know this is going to sound cold, but it doesn't matter if it was eighty-nine times or just one. It doesn't matter that Natalie cut off Kim Zwillich's fingers. Mr. Jefferies disagrees with me; he says that's exactly what matters to a jury. While that might be true, I don't think it's right. Dead is dead.

But I understand all your readers will want the nasty details. That's what makes it fun for them. I mean, I love the thing in *The Gunslinger* where he goes into the town and the people turn on him and he just slices them up in that big battle. I like those big battles. You get to go way overboard with those little gross-out details. I figure that's what you'll want to do here. I'm not sure how you'll do that with real people because it would be hard on their families, but if it's fiction I guess it doesn't matter. You can just change their names. Nobody believes the people in your books are real anyway. That's what makes it fun.

90

To get the combination—at least that's what happened with Kim Zwillich. With Margo Styles, I couldn't tell you why. I know being in there right then made me feel like everything had gone crazy, like I couldn't be part of this even though I knew I was. It was a weird kind of high, like when you're driving and you realize you're driving and have been for a while. I don't know why she did it. Maybe because she's a crazy, evil person.

And you know who does it in her book, don't you? She has me looking at her the whole time too, like I wanted to do the same things to her. And people believe it because it makes sense, there's some kind of motive behind it. Why she did it is just a mystery.

We were all angry about Lamont getting shot, but that didn't stop me from feeling bad for the girls and for Reggie Tyler and even for Victor Nunez, who kind of started it all. I didn't want anyone else to get hurt. I just wanted to lock them in the freezer and get the heck out of there.

91

Lamont shot them, but first something really funny happened. The sprinkler system went off.

I guess the smoke was bad enough to trigger it. We were standing at the door of the freezer, and it nailed us. I knew that when it went off, it automatically called the fire department.

"Great," Lamont said, and stepped into the freezer. This is where I gave him my gun because his clip was empty. This is where the prosecution said I was lying and called on Natalie to prove it. All right, I'll admit that I did use the knife a little—after Natalie had—and that maybe I hit Mr. Close for trying to run over Lamont, but I never shot anybody. Never.

First Lamont shot Margo Styles and then Kim Zwillich. I guess he was hoping Donald Anderson would remember the combination. He didn't. Lamont shot him in the face and then the chest to make sure.

Water was pouring from the ceiling, hissing on the grill. Up front, the Order-Matic was going nuts. I grabbed my shirt and my purse and on my way out a plastic cup with the morning's tips in it. We walked out the front door, soaking wet, Lamont bleeding, like no one would notice.

92

They were dead when we left, I'm positive. In court they showed pictures of them frozen together from the water, and none of them had moved. I'm sure a bunch of guys had to pick them up and take them out of the freezer so they'd thaw. Either that or they chipped them out with an ice pick. Either way it's a lousy job, and I feel sorry that people had to do that.

93

I'd say we got about fifteen dollars from the register, ten from Margo Styles's changemaker, and another two from the tip cup. So about twenty-seven dollars. It was enough to buy us some gas and a diet Pepsi for everybody.

In the paper they always call the murders senseless. They were messed up maybe, but there was a reason at least.

Another thing is they call us serial killers. That's just inaccurate—a serial killer kills one person a whole bunch of times. The other thing that bugs me is spree killers. I don't think that's right either. Spree makes it sound like it was a good time, like we were happy-go-lucky or something, like we were having fun, when really it was the exact opposite of that.

94

The Roadrunner was fine, except a Satellite pulled into the stall beside it, so we had to wait to get in. Gainey was asleep, still holding the spoon in his hand. He'd slopped his ice cream all over the seat and Natalie sat right in it; I'd forgotten to get napkins. Lamont's one arm wasn't working and he had to close his door twice. The engine kicked over on its first try, like always; there wasn't any suspense.

I checked my mirrors and looked through the Satellite to see if anyone was coming, then I eased out and rolled around the back of the building. It had a door with a square window with chicken wire in the glass, but I couldn't see anything. The sprinklers must have taken care of the smoke; I didn't hear any fire engines yet. We coasted past the blonde in the Camaro and the guy still reading in the Tempest. When I stopped to turn left across traffic, I had to wait for a Jimmy to pull in. The bank clock across the way said it was eleven-thirty. We'd only been in there fifteen minutes.

I slid into traffic. It didn't look like we were going to make the light, so I changed lanes and pulled a right on red and headed east on 66. Natalie leaned over the front seat to check on Lamont. She lifted his shirt. I had to watch the road.

"How's he doing?" I said.

"It hurts," Lamont said.

"He'll be okay," Natalie said. "It went all the way through but I don't think it hit anything important. There'd be a lot more blood."

"We should get him to a doctor," I said.

"Maybe in Texas," she said.

"Why are we going this way?" Lamont said, a little out of breath.

"I just wanted to get away from there. I'll turn up here in a little."

I looked over and Natalie had taken her shirt off and was dabbing at his ribs, swabbing the blood off. It didn't look so bad when it was clean; it had almost stopped bleeding.

"How's that?" Natalie said.

"Thank you," he said, like after we made love, like he was glad to be that tired.

I looked back to the road and sped up, thinking it wasn't right. He was *my* husband, I thought. That should have been my job.

95

Traffic was light for the most part. We turned north on Coltrane, then headed west again.

We did see one Edmond cop going into a Braum's for lunch, a big old black-and-white Caprice. Natalie sat back so he wouldn't see her in her bra. You could make a big deal of it, like we were nervous, but we were just glad to be out of there. We were feeling lucky, kind of high because everything had been so crazy. The day was nice and we had enough money to get us to New Mexico. We passed the Braum's and made the next light, and Lamont laughed, and then Natalie, and even I started in then.

That's in Natalie's book too, but she makes it sound like she was shocked, like me and Lamont were bloodthirsty or something, which isn't true. It was just good to be moving.

96

We stopped at a Phillips 66 just over the tracks by the Purina grain elevator. I pulled up to the far pump so no one would see us. For a minute I thought of pulling a drive-off but we didn't want any attention.

Lamont always got the premium, like it made a difference.

"You guys want anything to drink?" I asked while it was filling. I figured Gainey would want some juice when he woke up.

I don't remember what the total was, but we had enough if you included the change. I went to the booth to pay and the guy behind the counter was drawing something in a notebook, bending over it so his nose was an inch away from the paper. It was a picture of the planets lining up. It was Mister Fred Fred.

I didn't want him to recognize me, so I turned my head sideways and tipped it so I could hide behind my hair. I slid the bills with the change on top into the trough and he punched up the sale. He didn't even look he was so far gone. It was too easy, old Mister Fred Fred.

"Bye!" I said.

He didn't even look up from the page. It was disappointing. I went around the side and got some Pepsis from the machine.

"Hey," I said in the car, "guess who that was," but neither of them remembered him. I wondered if anybody had ever listened to me.

Mister Fred Fred—that's it for him. I thought they'd call him in to ID me to put me at the scene, but they never did. They probably wouldn't of believed him even if he did remember me. I have no idea what happened to him, whether the space rays got him or not. In a way, I think they already had.

We also stopped at a rest area off U.S. 270 to wash Lamont and get him into some fresh clothes. We cleaned the seats and threw his bloody jeans and Margo Styles's shirt into a trash barrel. I tried to light it on fire but the wind was too strong. Lamont said it felt like a stomachache or just a bad stitch. He could make a fist, but it hurt to raise the arm.

"You don't mind driving," he asked.

"You think I'd let her?" I said, and he smiled. There were still some things we agreed on. Maybe not enough, but some.

And we stopped in the lot of a drugstore just over the Texas line in a little town called Higgins. I changed Gainey and gave him his juice and a few saltines and we pooled the money left to buy Lamont a bottle of peroxide and a big gauze bandage. Me and Natalie fought over who got to go in, and finally I did.

Nowhere else close to Oklahoma though, we were very care-ful. I don't know if Lamont had a plan, or Natalie, but I didn't. I guess we were just hoping things would go our way. We had no money, Lamont was shot, and we'd been awake for two days. The only thing going for us was we had a fast car and a good-sized bag of crank. We were dumb to think that might be enough.

97

Why did we go west? I don't know. It was never a question. I guess we figured the land was big enough to hide us, or that there might be something better out there, a new start. Isn't that what the old Okies hoped for? In school we had to read *The Grapes of Wrath*. This wasn't much different. There wasn't anything going on in Kansas or Arkansas, and being from Oklahoma, we'd go to Heck before we went to Texas. West was really the only choice.

Sometimes I'll sit down with my atlas and follow the roads we took, and I'll think, there, that's where we should of split off south, or maybe if we'd taken the route through the mountains, or that dirt road across the desert. It doesn't do any good, but I do it. And I see all the sights again—the tumbleweeds caught in the guardrails, the Navajo trading posts with rugs hanging from the porch rafters, the hippie hitchhikers with jugs of water yoked around their necks. I see the wind-bent trees around broken-down homesteads, and the sagging beehives out back, I see the armadillos crushed on the road and the green bridges advertising their height. But when I try to see all of us in the car, it's always those last few miles outside of Shiprock, the dust filling the back window. It's sad—I've got all of Texas and most of New Mexico, but all I remember is Shiprock.

Here's something you'll like. If we'd have kept going on that road we would have ended up at the Four Corners, where the states come together at a plaque. Here's the choice I would've had: Utah still shoots people; Arizona and Colorado have the gas chamber; at the time, New Mexico electrocuted you, now they've changed to lethal injection. The state police say I was less than thirty miles short of it. Mr. Jefferies would have had one tough decision to make.

Why west? It's the way you go out here. It's like "Route 66," the song—*it winds from Chicago to L.A.* No one goes the other way. It would be stupid.

98

We were halfway across the Texas panhandle when we heard it— Dumas, maybe even Dalhart. For miles there was nothing but fence, gates onto grazing land, cattle guards in the middle of the road. In the distance, the grain elevators rose like white hotels, announcing the towns. It was dinnertime and the sun was in my eyes. We'd gotten fifty dollars from these teenagers in a parking lot in Pampa for an eighth. We gassed up in Skellytown, I snorted a few lines and we headed north. The plan was for Lamont and Natalie to get some rest. They were just getting settled when it came over the radio—three suspects, a yellow older-model Plymouth. They read our license plate number and gave our names, all except Gainey.

"Where the heck did they get all that?" Lamont said.

"Heck," Natalie said. "Heck."

"Do you want me to stop or something?" I said.

"No," Lamont said.

"How far is it to Mexico?" Natalie asked, and Lamont handed her the map. He said he was fine now except he couldn't feel his hand. Natalie rattled the map open.

"Well?" I said.

"It's far."

99

All night and all the next day. That's how I got my nickname, the Speed Queen. Lucinda always makes fun of it; she says it's a kind of washing machine. I don't mind it. I was thinking you might use it for a title. *The Speed Queen Confesses*, how's that sound?

But yeah, driving all night up and down those two-lanes, cruising through the little four-corners towns. It was Saturday night and the kids were out low-riding in their chopped Hondas and frenched Chevy Luvs. It was slow going. Lamont and Natalie were sleeping, so was Gainey. All the drive-ins were jammed. They reminded me of Coit's and the good times we had there. Every little cow town had one—the Dairy Princess, Custard's Last Stand, the Dallas Dairyette—the kids in sweatshirts in the back of pickup trucks, couples dating in flame-jobbed fastbacks, sucking down fizzes and splits and dipsy-doodles. I thought about how easy their lives were, and how messed up they'd get, and then I'd hit the town limits and click on my high beams and make time.

Further west in Texas, the towns were closed for the night, only roadside diners open—the Wide-A-Wake, the Miss Ware City—their signs trying to convince me I wanted KC steaks and broasted chicken and chiliburgers and spudnuts. *Coldest beer in town!* one place claimed, but it had a telephone number written in white shoe polish across the front windows. *Livestock auction every Tuesday.* We passed the shells of old drive-ins, hollow train stations, a gas station advertising used tires, and then for the next fifty miles nothing but stars and maybe an iguana caught in my lights.

We hit the New Mexico border after midnight and I fixed the clock and it was Saturday again. You could smell the feed yards coming. I had gum and I turned the radio on low just to have someone to listen to. The night hypnotizes you, the lines holding the car on the road, the reflectors tricking your eyes. Cattle trucks passed the other way, deadheading, lit up like UFOs. On the sharper curves people had left shrines for loved ones, plastic flowers and yellow ribbons nailed on crosses. It was a stretch you'd fall asleep on during the day—nothing for miles, then a graying billboard, a mileage sign for old mining ghost towns and places you'd never heard of: Capulin and Wagon Mound, Ojo del Madre. Around three in the morning, in the middle of the desert, a railroad gate swung down in front of us and a Santa Fe engine blared past, hauling a long line of gondola cars. An hour later I had to wait for it again. It was like we were going nowhere.

At Springer the road finally hit I-25, and I pulled into a Loaf 'n Jug and while I was filling up, squeegeed the bugs off the windshield and bought a cold six of diet Pepsi. Gainey woke up and I gave him a Nilla wafer. I got back on the road and chugged a can and felt better. When I turned around, he was out again, the cookie in his fist.

The mountains slowed us down. They were scenic, like it said on the map, but the curves took hours and hurt my eyes. Dawn came up. Lamont's bandage was dry, Natalie was wearing one of my shirts. The shadows of the trees fluttered over their faces, and I tried not to think of Kim Zwillich and Margo Styles. Outside of Taos we got stuck behind a Winnebago with black nylon skirts; on the spare they had a map of the country with all the states colored in, and I thought that would be a neat thing to do, just keep going till we hit all of them.

"You want me to drive?" Lamont asked when he got up. His hand was better, he said, and showed me he could open and close it.

"I'm fine," I said. "Want a pop?"

In back, Natalie groaned and stretched her arms over her head. "Where the heck are we?"

"Cuba," I said. "The next town is fifty miles."

"I'm hungry," she said.

"I should eat something," Lamont said, like it was final.

"Something quick," I warned him.

We cruised through town, skipping the Tip Top Cafe and the Stagecoach Inn. There was nothing with a drive-thru, so I pulled in behind Anita's Coffee Pot. *Breakfast 99¢,* it said in the window. It was a trucker's cafe with desert scenes painted on the walls— knotty pine and gingham curtains and wagon-wheel chandeliers. The men sitting at the counter kept their baseball caps and jackets on. A twin Jetspray sent endless curtains of lemonade and fruit punch waterfalling down its sides. The waitress gave us a dangerous-looking high chair for Gainey. In the middle of the table there was a special holder for those jam packets with the foil lids. She gave us our menus and our water and said she'd be right back.

The menu was huge. Silver dollar pancakes, flannel cakes, pork fritters. Country ham, dropped eggs, buttered toast. They had dinner for breakfast—Adobe Pie and Zuni stew, chalupas and tamales and flautas, chilaquiles and stuffed sopaipillas and Hopiburgers, and for dessert, Millionaire Ice Box Pie. I wasn't hungry at all.

"Then just get coffee," Lamont said.

"This is stupid," I said.

"Marjorie, we have to eat."

"No," I said, "we have to not get caught. They'll feed us all sorts of stuff in jail."

Natalie just sat there reading the menu like she didn't have an opinion.

"You're just loving this," I said.

"Did I say anything?" she said.

"Forget it."

"I think someone's getting a little paranoid," she said.

"What do you mean someone?" I said. "I'm right here, Natalie. I'm not someone."

"Do you want people looking at us?" Lamont said. "Because that's what they're going to do if you don't control yourself."

"Look who's talking about control."

"Do you want to go sit in the car? Do you want me to treat you like a little kid? I'm not feeling too good if you haven't noticed. I don't need this stuff."

I said the F-word then and walked out. He could feed Gainey. They could be their own little family.

In the car I cracked my last diet Pepsi. It was warm. I didn't need them, I thought. They were my whole problem. And watching the cars passing behind me on the highway, I thought I could just take off and ditch the car somewhere and start over.

But I couldn't. They needed me to drive.

100

We were on 44 in the middle of nowhere. We'd come down out of the mountains into the high desert. There were red buttes everywhere, and adobe ruins, and sage. I was hoping to see a real roadrunner, kind of a good omen. We were in the Apache reservation because we passed a fry bread and jewelry stand set up by the tribe with a big sign. Lamont wanted to stop for some cheap cigarettes but I said forget it. I don't know where I thought I was going, I just had to move.

I'd never seen a real reservation, and all the trailers and junked cars surprised me. I thought they got money from the government.

Out in the desert there were no fences, only a string of low telephone poles beside a railroad line. *Gusty wind likely,* a sign said. I had the Roadrunner opened up in fourth and just humming. That big Hemi was worth every penny. The dips lifted us off the road, made your stomach jump. Off to our right, crows perched on the phone poles, waiting.

"Not much out here," Lamont said.

And just then I looked up and saw the cop car in the mirror, gaining on us. It wasn't a state trooper because they had Crown Vics, and this was an old Fury, probably one some other police force sold when they got their new ones. It was just luck—it was the only engine out there that had a chance against us. It was going to be two big Mopars going head to head. I'd take him, no question, even if I didn't know the road.

"Cop," I said.

Lamont didn't turn to look. "You're sure."

"No," I said, "it's Mr. Softee doing one-ten. Of course I'm sure."

"Does he have his lights on?"

"He just put them on."

"Pull over," Lamont said.

"What?" I said, and we started to argue. Now that I look back on it, I realize I should have fought him harder. But it's too late now.

You want to hear a weird one? In Switzerland they used to put you in a box and saw you in half. I don't know why.

101

I'd say he was around five-seven, a hundred and sixty. His wrists were thick like a drummer's. He had black hair parted on the left, or the right; I can't remember because most of the time I was watching him in the sideview mirror. His uniform was khaki, like the Marines. He must have had black shoes or boots, I can't remember. He had a gun, but he hadn't taken it out, he'd only unsnapped his holster like they teach you to do.

Lamont slipped the .45 from the glove compartment and hid it beneath his right leg.

I don't know how to describe Lloyd Red Deer's face. Round, kind of like a pumpkin. He had brown eyes and his cheeks had little pits in the skin. No mustache. Yellow teeth from smoking. He came up on my side and looked in, and I could tell he had no idea, that no one had told him about us. It was kind of funny but sad too. He said, "Afternoon," to be polite.

"Ma'am," he said, "do you know how fast you were going?"

"No, sir," I said. Did I say he had gloves on? He did, white ones like a crossing guard. It was cute.

"I'm going to have to ask you for your license and registration," he said, and I turned to Lamont and said, "Honey?" like he'd get them for me.

102

Lamont shot him. He leaned forward and opened the glove compartment like he was looking for the papers, then he spun toward Lloyd Red Deer with the gun in his other hand. I shied back so it wouldn't hit me. For a second he didn't shoot and I thought he'd forgotten the safety. Then I realized it was his bad hand.

Lloyd Red Deer went for his gun, I don't know why. All he had to do was duck.

Lamont switched hands and shot him, and at the same time Lloyd Red Deer shot Lamont. It knocked Lamont's head against the window and the gun dropped on the floor.

His eyes were closed. I grabbed him by the shoulders. The bullet had made a hole in his shirt pocket and Lamont was gasping. The blood pulsed out. Natalie had ahold of him too. She was screaming so I couldn't think and I shoved her into the backseat. She must of sat on Gainey because he started wailing.

I ripped the bandage off Lamont's ribs and pressed it against his chest. Natalie wouldn't stop.

"Shut the heck up!" I said. I grabbed her by the hair and stuck her hand over the bandage. "Hold this!"

I tore Lamont's shirt off and leaned him forward. The bullet was still in there. I thumbed back his lids; his eyes were just whites. He made slurping sounds when he breathed. I didn't want to believe he was going to die so I pretended he was just knocked out from hitting the window. Slurp, he was going, slurp. Gainey was crying and my mind couldn't hold on to anything. "Okay," I kept saying, like I had a thought. We'd get him somewhere and let him rest and he'd be fine. "Right," I said. "Okay. Just keep holding that."

I checked on Lloyd Red Deer. He was lying on his side in the road, and I could see the outline of a wallet in his back pocket. I looked across the desert; there was no one coming, so I jumped out.

"What are you doing?" Natalie said.

"Just hold that against him," I said.

I got back in and got the car started.

"Where are we going?" Natalie sobbed.

"I don't know!" I said. "Stop asking me questions!"

103

He was definitely dead when we left him. Lamont shot him straight in the face with his .45. He had a hat, one of those Smokey the Bear deals with the strap in back, and it ended up across the road in a creosote bush.

I don't know anything about the shots to his body. They say they were from his own gun. Even if that *was* true, they didn't kill him. There wasn't much left of his head.

That's another one I hate—getting your head chopped off. Nobody does that anymore, at least not in this country. I remember those old movies with the guillotine, or the big guy with the bare chest and the black hood and the ax. They always give the prisoner a chance to say his last words, and while he's talking the king's pardon comes through, or his friends shoot an arrow right in the big guy's heart and a huge sword fight breaks out.

I don't think that's going to happen. Most of the people outside the gate tonight have signs like *Thank God It's Fryday* and *Roast in Peace.* They don't know what's going on, they don't know me at all, they just want to cheer when the lights dim at 12:01. *Buckle Up, Marjorie.* It's a tradition, the Deathwatch. A lot of frat boys come out and drink beer and make a nuisance of themselves—a lot of nuts. And they're all here to see me. It, really. I read that at the last public execution in the U.S., twenty thousand people showed up.

Even inside of here there's a lot of commotion. When they did that Connie gal, they locked us down and showed us videos until three in the morning. Etta Mae said she hoped they'd show one with Brad Pitt in it. Lucinda said she was holding out for Wesley Snipes. I knew they were just trying to lighten things up for me. "Tom Cruise," I said. "It'll be my going-away present."

All the kidding is like the names they have for it, they're supposed to make it easier. The gas chamber's The Big Sleep or The Time Machine. Sitting in the chair is Riding the Lightning. Getting hanged is just The Drop. There's nothing special for lethal injection, just what they call any execution—After Midnight, like the old Clapton tune. *After midnight, we gonna let it all hang out.* All week I've been listening to people whistle it, the way it echoes off the concrete, down the long halls. It's hard to like a tune when it comes at you that way, but I do.

104

I stopped at the closest motel, which wasn't until Farmington. The Dan-Dee Colonial Motel. The sign was an oversized coach light. It was almost dark when we pulled in; next to the office a blue bug zapper crackled. Natalie went in with some of the money from Lloyd Red Deer and came back with a key to room 8, the furthest one from the office. I don't know if she used an alias. She walked over while I followed in the car.

The room had a harpoon on the wall and paintings of whaling ships and men in rain slickers in dinghies. The lamps above the beds came out of miniature ship's wheels. I took Gainey in first, then both of us helped carry Lamont. You couldn't tell if he was breathing and the blood was still coming. We laid him on one of the beds and locked the door.

I pulled the bandage off and watched the wound fill up and run over. I pressed it back down again.

"Get some ice," I said—I don't know why—and Natalie found the bucket and unlocked the door again.

I checked his wrist and couldn't find anything and checked his neck. I leaned my ear down to his lips and then his chest. There was nothing, so I did it again, holding my breath to listen better. No.

I got up and put the chain on the door and picked up Gainey and touched his hand to Lamont's cheek. I put him back in the car seat and laid down next to Lamont like we were going to sleep, then I rolled over and held him close. The blood was still hot. I thought if I held him long enough he'd open his eyes and say everything was fine.

Natalie knocked on the door like it was a secret.

"I love you," I said, and kissed him and held him tight against me.

Natalie knocked.

I kissed him a last time and ran my fingers over his teeth, his pretty fangs.

Natalie knocked again.

"Hold on!" I said, and got up and opened the door.

She looked at my front all covered with blood, and Gainey's jumper, and she knew. She put the bucket on the night table and knelt down beside him.

"Why did you lock the door?" she said. "Why did you lock the door?"

So yes, that part of her book is true.

It reminded me of my dad. This was on Kickingbird Circle. A bunch of friends were over. It was summer and we were in the backyard, running through the sprinklers. My mom was in her garden; she had her gloves on and her shears. My dad had these striped swim trunks with a string that tied in the front. He was chasing us through the spray, and when I looked back to see where he was, he was lying facedown on the ground. The water arced over him and came back my way.

"Get up," I said.

"Come on, Dad."

"Hey," I said. "Quit faking."

105

No, Lamont didn't have any last words.

Actually, the last thing he said was "Just do what I tell you." He said it to me, not her.

For the book, you could make "Not much out here" the last thing he says. Lamont would like that.

Wait a second.

Who is it?

Okay. Thanks, Janille.

It's Mr. Jefferies. This is probably it, since there's only twenty minutes left. Wish me luck.

It was him. They turned me down. Not enough new evidence for another trial.

What can you do, you know?

Yep.

So I guess I should finish this. For Gainey, and for Mr. Jefferies.

I'd like to call my mom.

Mr. Jefferies was funny. He said, "I've got some good news and I've got some bad news."

And I said, "What's the good news?"

And he said, "I was just kidding, there is no good news."

Here's a good one: when the firing squad shoots you, blood flies out of your mouth.

106

That same night.

I was still flying but Natalie had to crash. We left Lamont where he was. I said I'd sleep on the floor and she was so tired that she believed me. I watched the TV without sound for a while—something dumb, you can make something up. Around midnight I went into the bathroom and did another three lines off the edge of the sink. The light from the TV made the pattern of the wallpaper jump out like a test pattern. I looked in a mirror for a little until I couldn't stand it. I went outside to the car and got the .45 and a box of shells. It was cool out, and the neon turned my skin a pretty blue. I went back into the bathroom and loaded the gun and snorted another four lines and washed my face. I took a big breath in the mirror.

"Okay," I said.

I took the pillow from Lamont's bed and walked over to Natalie. The lights were out and the TV was running all over the walls. I stood there and looked down at her for a while—at her hair and her arms, her perfect nails. I thought of our mornings with her toys and how I'd never felt so desirable, so alive inside my skin. I looked over at Lamont and thought about them being found together; I didn't want that.

Just then the show cut to a commercial and the screen went black, leaving me in the dark. When it came back, Natalie was looking straight at me.

I shoved the gun against her chest and fired. I completely forgot about the pillow; the sound made Gainey scream. Natalie rolled off the bed, knocking the bucket off the night table. The water splashed over her back. You could see the hole the bullet made where it came out. I didn't think I had to check.

"Liar," I said.

I threw the covers over her and started packing.

When I had everything together, I went out and unlocked the car. We were the only car in the lot. The road was empty. I went back in and wrapped Lamont in the bedspread and grabbed him under the arms and hauled him across the carpet and through the door and pushed him halfway into the backseat. I had to go around the other side and drag the rest of him in, and by then I was sweating.

I dragged Natalie out the same way and muscled her up and into the trunk. Then I got the bags and buckled Gainey's car seat in beside me. He was still squealing. I kept my lights off until I was a quarter mile or so down the road. When I flicked them on, the white lines shot off in front of me like a runway, but I knew I really wasn't going anywhere.

Remember *The Great Escape*, with Steve McQueen jumping the barbed wire on his motorcycle? Any of those movies where they tunnel out using spoons and homemade sleds you have to lie down on. They never know where to put the dirt. You're always rooting for them to get out, even when they're somewhere like Alcatraz. You don't really worry about what they did to get in because they're always innocent. But I was driving along then, through the desert, and I passed this sign that said, *Hitchhikers may be escaped prisoners,* and the first thing I did was lock Gainey's door.

107

I have no idea where it was, I just knew I had to get rid of her. It was dark, so I slowed down until I found some tire tracks going off into the desert. I turned on my high beams and the Roadrunner bumped over the ruts. The tracks went on for miles, but I figured they were Jeeps, and I didn't want to get the back end hung up on something. I watched the odometer. When I was five miles from the road, I stopped and killed the lights.

The thing about the desert is you can hear for miles. I stepped out into the darkness and I could hear a train clanking way off in the distance. I opened the trunk and the little bulb on the inside of the lid blinded me.

Natalie had shifted; her face rested on a yellow jug of anti-freeze like it was a pillow. There was blood on the rug and the spare. I wrestled her out, but she hung up on the lip. Her shirt was caught in the lock. I had to let go and it ripped and she rolled into my legs and almost knocked me over. I closed the lid so no one would see us. I dragged her off the road a ways, thinking I'd throw some sand over her, but it was dirt and hurt my fingers.

So the whole buried-alive thing is a joke. Left for dead I can buy, even if it was only one shot, but calling it a miracle makes me angry. It's a miracle I didn't try to kill her before that for what she did to me.

And then the whole thing gets stupid because I try to do a three-point turn and get stuck and when I finally rock myself out, I follow the wrong tracks and get lost. Cattle are wandering through my headlights. This could be funny or sad or me just getting what I deserve. It's your choice.

108

Four or five hours, because it wasn't until daylight that I found a road. If you look on the map you'll see it south of Farmington, a dotted gray line headed west off of 371. It's dirt and breaks down when it hits the littlest wash. It takes you into the big Navajo reservation about forty miles north of Window Rock and finally hooks up with Route 666. I thought you'd like that.

I was low on gas and Gainey needed breakfast so I made sure the covers were on Lamont and stopped at a Love's Country Store. Big ristras of chiles hung by the pumps. The Roadrunner was red with dust; Lamont would of had a heart attack. A couple of snowbirds were filling up their RVs and there were Christmas decorations in the windows. The diet Pepsis I bought had penguins on them, and all the beer cartons said *Seasons Greetings*. On the counter was a rack you could turn with different postcards of Shiprock. I read the back of some while I waited in line.

The Navajos believed the rock was a magic ship that would help them escape their enemies when they were in danger. According to the legend, it had brought the entire tribe here from a far-off land, kind of like Battlestar Galactica. Another one said the mountain was a sacred burial site, like a stairway to heaven, and that warriors buried on the rock were raised into the spirit world. They had keychains too, and wallet kits with the picture of the silhouette embossed on leather.

The attendant had long hair and a Joy Division T-shirt. He gave me too much change and I told him so.

"Thanks," he said. "Nice car."

After they caught me, I wondered if he'd turned me in. I don't think so. I'm pretty sure it was the girl at the park.

109

Not much, it's pretty empty. Mountains on both sides. Cliffs, arroyos, the tailings from abandoned mines. Some old trading posts falling in on themselves, maybe an RV park. The Navajos had their own roads coming off 666, but most of them were gravel and on the map they didn't meet up with anything.

I pulled off at a historical marker to feed Gainey his peaches and do two quick lines. There was still a good corner of the bag left. While I was laying out the second one, I saw Shiprock across the desert, the sun hitting the top part.

I forgot what I was doing for a minute. It did look like a ship, way up above everything, the way you think of Noah's Ark after it runs aground. You could see why they hoped it would float away and take them back where they came from. There was nothing to stick around here for; it was dead land—just rocks and scrub, hawks and lizards. No water at all.

110

I didn't have a plan, I just got the idea of Shiprock in my head. I knew I couldn't drive around with Lamont in the backseat forever, so when I saw the state park sign, I slowed down and turned off.

I don't know what you'd call it—Indian 33? In my atlas the number's inside an arrowhead, so I don't know.

My plan right then was to take Lamont to Shiprock and bury him somewhere. For being awake five straight days, it wasn't that bad a decision.

After that, I have no idea. Arizona? California? If I'd of been thinking, I would of made a run for Mexico. But I wasn't. I didn't know what I was doing. Just driving.

111

It was off of 33, inside the park entrance. You had to pay two dollars at a log cabin booth. The girl there gave me a foldout brochure with a map on it. I figure she's the one who called because I stopped in the parking lot to see where I was going. The place was deserted except for a guy fitting bags into the trash cans. She must of heard about Lloyd Red Deer over the radio. On the map you could go two ways. I just sat there like a dummy trying to decide while she wrote down my license plate.

I went right. The road switchbacked up the side of the mountain. You were supposed to go ten miles an hour around the turns. I went as far as I could go. The road stopped at an overlook with a low stone wall and a laminated map of what you were looking at. The drop was about a thousand feet and it was all red rock. We were still a half mile from Shiprock itself, but I figured it was close enough.

I flipped my seat up and grabbed Lamont under the arms. You'd think he'd smell but he didn't, just the blood did. I hauled him across the lot and leaned him against the wall. It was a clear morning and I could see my breath coming quick. I took the covers away from his face. The brushburn was just healing. I closed my eyes and put my forehead against his, the way we did when we needed to talk. Birds were chirping, and chipmunks in the rocks. I told him I'd miss him and I'd always be his. I'd take care of Gainey and his car. Then I rolled him over the edge and walked away.

When I got back in, Gainey was clapping his hands.

"What are you doing?" I said, and poked him in the tummy. "What do you think you're doing, huh?"

112

They were waiting for me inside the park entrance, four of them parked sideways across the road in pairs so I couldn't ram them. I didn't see the helicopter until later. I slowed down and then stopped in the lot.

"Driver," one of them said over a speaker. "Put your hands where we can see them.

"Driver. Roll down your window and hold out your hands."

I had a full tank of gas and they were in Crown Vics. I punched the clutch in and swung around. In the mirror I could see them scrambling and slamming their doors.

I didn't want to deal with the hairpins again, and took the other fork, hoping it might go somewhere. I flapped the map open. It was another overlook. Through the pines I could see them coming after me.

The view was the same here—Shiprock with the orange morning sun on it. I pulled into a space by the wall like it was a drive-in movie. I unbuckled Gainey and held him on my lap, smelling his hair and his skin, and we sat there waiting for them.

113

No, but I could have. I still had the .45 in the glove compartment. I couldn't with Gainey there. I didn't want to anyway.

They pulled up short of us and blocked the road again. The same guy did the thing over the speaker. I could barely hear with the helicopter.

I kissed Gainey on the top of the head and buckled him into his car seat, then I turned off the car and rolled down the window and put out my hands.

"Now open the door from the outside," he said, and I did.

"Now step out. Let me see your hands."

I got out and looked at them, seven or eight all hiding behind their cars.

"Turn around," he said. "Now lift your shirt."

I did and the air was chilly on my skin.

"Now put your hands in the air."

Hold on. Sorry.

Five?

Okay, I'm on the next-to-last one.

That's Janille, she thought we might have one last bag of Funyuns. I still have to call my mom. I'd like to pray too, if you don't mind.

I bet they're cheering outside. Fine, I forgive them.

Do you want all that stuff? I don't think it's that interesting. They basically made me lie down on the cold road with my hands spread wide over my head, then they came and this tall guy kneeled on my neck. They thought someone else might be in the car even though I told them it was just a baby. They snuck up on it with their guns drawn. While they had me down, they took Gainey away to another car. He was screaming, and the cop wasn't even holding him right. I got upset and someone grabbed my hair. Someone else hit me in the kidney and I thought I'd barf. They thought it was funny how much I was struggling. They were laughing.

"Where's your friends?" they said. "Your friends take off on you?"

When they threw me against the hood they split my chin open. The woman who patted me down bent my arm so high behind my back she separated my shoulder.

The pain made me dizzy and I began to cry.

"Does that hurt?" she said.

"Yes," I said.

"Too bad."

In the car, the two officers told me what they'd do to me if it was up to them. Looking back, it would have been quicker.

That's it, that's the end. It's not as good as Natalie wandering along the road with her shirt all bloody and the Indian family coming by in their beat-up pickup, I know that. I don't know what you can do about it though.

In the movies the death scene's always a big ending, so you could do that. It's not that dramatic in real life, but that's okay. People don't want real life anyway, it's boring.

Did you see that Sharon Stone movie last year where she gets executed? It was stupid but she was good. I like her a lot, but she's too perfect to be me. I don't know who you'll have to get — someone young. And if it's possible I'd like Keanu Reeves to be Lamont.

114

Last one. Finally.

Do I have any last words?

I don't believe anything is the last because I believe in eternity. I believe I'll be saved and that I'll live in Jesus Christ forever. Amen.

That's a pretty good last word — amen.

Before I go I'd just like to thank Mr. Jefferies again for believing in me, and Janille and Sister Perpetua for helping me on my personal journey.

I'd like to say to Gainey, when you hear this, try not to judge us. Take your mom's mistakes to heart and learn from them. I love you and so does your daddy. I'm kissing your picture right now. I'll have it with me always.

As for you, I'd like to thank you again for all the money and for being interested in my story in the first place. Good luck with the book. I hope it's a good one. I'm sure it'll put Natalie's to shame. I'm counting on it.

Wait a sec.

I hear you.

Okay, I've got to go. Janille's got her keys out and the execution team's ready. The witnesses are inside. It's time.

I wish Mr. Jefferies was here.

I wonder what it's like outside, if they've started honking their horns and flashing their lights yet. They'll be happy at least. Give them what they want, right?

I'm sure my mom's got the radio on. I love you, Mom.

I'm coming.

When you come out, talk to Darcy and Etta Mae, and don't listen to Lucinda. Garlyn and Joy can help you out with the early stuff.

Just remember, everything I've told you is true. I'm completely innocent.

Try to be nice to me, okay?

Just tell a good story.